M000200414

Modern Times

Modern Times

Cathy Sweeney

WEIDENFELD & NICOLSON

First published in the Republic of Ireland in 2020 by The Stinging Fly Press

This edition published in Great Britain 2020 by Weidenfeld & Nicolson
an imprint of The Orion Publishing Group Ltd
Carmelite House, 50 Victoria Embankment
London EC4Y 0DZ

An Hachette UK Company

1 3 5 7 9 10 8 6 4 2

Earlier versions of these stories appeared in:
*Banshee, The Dublin Review, Egress, Meridian, Winter Papers,
Young Irelanders, The Stinging Fly and Stinging Fly Stories.*
'Flowers in Water' was broadcast on BBC Radio 4.

A CIP catalogue record for this book is
available from the British Library.

ISBN (Hardback) 978 1 4746 1848 9
ISBN (eBook) 978 1 4746 1850 2
ISBN (Audio) 978 1 4746 1859 5

Printed in Great Britain by Clays Ltd, Elcograf S.p.A.

www.weidenfeldandnicolson.co.uk
www.orionbooks.co.uk

To JL

Contents

Modern Times

A Love Story

There once was a woman who loved her husband's cock so much that she began taking it to work in her lunchbox. It was early in the marriage and the husband had not yet decided what his wife could have and what she could not—they were still in love—and so he went along with her little peccadillo. In the mornings, after the man had showered, the wife would take the cock and wrap it in cling film and put it in her lunchbox alongside her bratwurst sandwich, portion of fruit, and chocolate biscuit— everyone needs a treat! In the evenings when she returned from work the wife would matter-of-factly return the cock to her husband before preparing their evening meal—venison stew or beef casserole or sometimes the husband's favourite, the French dish called chicken-in-wine. It was no doubt an unusual arrangement but right up until the husband filed for divorce it seemed to suit both parties. Of course, the divorce lawyers went to town about a cock in a lunchbox and there was some unsavoury press coverage. When it was all over the wife got a new job in a new town and took up pottery. She became very good at it and exhibitions of her work were held biannually. The husband married the woman he had fallen in love with. She was young and modern and had no need of his or anyone else's cock, thank you very much. The funny thing was that years later, when the husband occasionally put his hand to his crotch and found his cock firmly in place, he experienced an intense but fleeting nostalgia for the good old days.

The Woman With Too Many Mouths

I met the woman with too many mouths in the plaza at the start of summer. It was a warm night and it smelled of melted grass. I would not normally have noticed such a woman, but I was in a mood where each step took me further into the realm where even the drift of a stranger's cigarette smoke suggested life both as it is and as it should be; and it was in this mood that the woman caught my attention. She was not my type: a crooked nose, legs marbled with muscle, gulag eyes. But as I saw her on that night of warm grass, she possessed a strange beauty. Only subsequently did I discover that the woman had too many mouths.

In life you rarely get what you want; you desire brown eyes and marry a girl with eyes of sky. The woman with too many mouths was almost ugly. Her beauty depended on the angle of the moon, on her perception of my perception, and so on. But her mouth, it must be said, had no truck with subjectivity. I spoke to her that night on the plaza. *It's a lovely evening*. She answered and rain came from her mouth. Nothing unusual there, you say, and you are right. It was ordinary rain, soft and seasonless. I was dispirited. And that is why, some weeks later, when the woman lying beneath me—we were picnicking in the country—breathed hay onto my white shirt, it was so unexpected. I had ironed the shirt with great difficulty, the linen having been left too long in the sun, and watched transfixed as the fresh hay, reeking faintly of cattle and fertiliser, billowed against it before being carried away in the breeze.

I planned to end my association with the woman. She was, as I have said, not my type. But some nights later, moths—not two but twenty, the ones you think are butterflies until someone says otherwise—flew out of the woman's mouth and around my bathroom. The woman had gone in there to douche. When she screamed I thought there must be a spider in the closet and it was with irritation that I uttered, *I'm coming, I'm coming*, and finally turned the handle on the bathroom door. In distress, the woman was strangely beautiful; each moth flew from her mouth unique, blue and timburalis, magenta and persimmon. I put my arms around the woman and we stood for a long time, shadowed here and there by tiny flickerings.

The woman asked me to hit her. Nothing original in that, you say, and you are right. I have of course hit women before, as hard or as soft as they wished, but when I went to strike the woman I lost all strength in the surface tension of air. I was shaken— not to be able to hit a woman is as bad as not being able to make love. I said to myself, *Dimitri, you are thirty-two years old. This woman is a fleeting glimpse of life. The world will always want servants but what the world needs is writers.* These thoughts—of the world and of writing—filled me with such a sense of destiny that I slept for days and when I woke I had forgotten all about the woman with too many mouths.

Weeks passed. I visited my dear friend in the city. My dear friend was absorbed with a countess and I with money, or more correctly the lack of it, and there were times, drinking coffee in the morning on the terrazzo, walking along the boulevard in the first cool of evening, when I had nothing to say to my dear friend and he had nothing to say to me, and so when the countess invited my dear friend to summer with her in the chateau, it was without sadness that we parted. To write my great novel I needed to think cold thoughts. I almost wished for winter.

I returned to the town and took a job as a typesetter, and because I knew nothing of typesetting, it was consuming. I got on with the other men, particularly a young man from the Balkans. We shared our cigarette breaks and took to drinking schnapps in the bars when the shift was over. The young man kept his money in his trouser pocket and when he stood up, coins fell to the floor. He had thick, black hair that he pushed from his face when I spoke to him, but left hanging when he spoke himself. I liked the young man, I liked the job, and the rest of the time I slept. If it wasn't for fate flapping in the background, I might have been happy. In one week, I received two telegrams. My dear friend had married the countess and my father had died, leaving me enough money to write my great novel.

I have not yet described to you the town in which I lived. It was a dead place. The surrounding countryside was flat and offered no vantage point from which a vision might arise; instead the town projected itself in recurring images of black and white. What little architecture existed was built from porous stone; in sun it glared and in rain it took on the appearance of sediment. Each street was an endless square around which people walked in straight lines, their faces dry from dry bread. I tell you this so that you will understand. It was not a place to write a great novel and so I accepted an invitation from my dear friend to visit him and his new wife in their chateau.

I could expend many pages recounting my time at the chateau: ten pages on scenery and mood, at least four on the charms of the countess, two on philosophical musings on the subject of friendship; but you would become bored, and worse, you would forget all about the woman with too many mouths. In summary, the countess enticed me into her world with ease until soon all thoughts were one question: were her breasts, swaddled in heavy damask, as small as they appeared to be? I was infatuated. My dear friend understood everything and found everything amusing, and so life at the chateau was a reverie of fat and thin emotions until one morning the countess announced she was with child. I returned to the town and found that, despite the hospitality of my hosts, I had very little money. All those evenings at the card table, watching the flattened breasts of the countess rise and fall, had been expensive.

I resumed my job as a typesetter and days again smeared into one another. The young man from the Balkans bought a wallet and developed a habit of taking it in and out of his pocket. I saw less of him. At night I sat at my desk drinking wine until thoughts fell into a frozen sleep. And then I saw her again, the woman with too many mouths. It was a cold night; the rain was endlessly vertical. In lamplight the woman's nose veered to the side and her arms were sinewed from carrying heavy buckets. We walked together through cobbled streets and each time my hand brushed hers, berries fell from her mouth: black and blue and crimson.

In my room the woman took off all her clothes and drank red cider until her mouth was swollen and her breath was sticky. Again she asked me to hit her and again I could not. We slept for days, far away from each other in the bed, and when I woke the woman with too many mouths was gone. Months passed. My dear friend who was wintering in the city came to visit. He had grown fat and suffered from heartburn. The countess was still luxurious, he told me, but always with child. At night we sat in hotel lounges drinking cocktails and smoking cigars. One evening while my dear friend lay slumped in an easy chair, I took comfort in a meretricious young girl from the countryside but at a crucial juncture I could not proceed. The downed hair of the girl's back had the texture of hay and her skin reeked faintly of cattle and fertiliser.

The experience of loss is not a sloped gradient; it is random black dots on an endless linear. At times, drinking with friends in cafés, laughing at the absurdity of this or that, questions printed themselves on my brain. *Did I love at all? Who can be sure whether he loves or not?* And I would forget all about the woman with too many mouths until hay poured once more like rain inside me.

And then I saw her again. The woman with too many mouths. They say coincidence is only for stories, and I am sure they are right, but the night I saw her smelled of melted grass and I was again in a mood of strange ascension. I sat down in the café beside her. The waiter fluttered by and I ordered a pastis. I raised my eyebrows but the woman shook her head, although her glass, I noticed, was almost empty. I lit a cigarette and drew my shoulders in. A passing stranger, glancing at the woman, could not have told from her body that a man was close to her. The smoke from my cigarette wafted into the woman's hair and she began to speak. As I listened, the tiniest flakes of whitened grey released themselves from her mouth, so light and casual, I thought I was seeing things. But I wasn't. As I inhaled, the woman exhaled. I squashed my half-smoked cigarette into the ashtray and the woman stopped speaking. The waiter arrived with the pastis and I drank the sweet liquid in one mouthful, stuck a note under the sugar bowl, and walked out into the night. The woman, to my surprise, came after me and in my room anchored herself to me, making waves of our bodies until I could no longer tell one from another. I kissed her mouth and ink came from it, staining the bed sheets and soaking through to the mattress. Again she asked me to hit her and this time I hit her on the mouth, harder and harder, until ink and blood were one and the woman with too many mouths disappeared.

Years passed. I wrote my great novel. I could write a hundred pages about writing my great novel, but who would read them? My novel was published. The reviews were favourable. It sold within expectation. And then nothing. What else is there?

What a ridiculous story, I hear you say. There are far greater torments in life than this! What about death or no money for boots or the violence that accompanies each age? I hear you say this and yet I do not turn my back when you spit in the dust and stamp on it.

A New Story Told Out Of An Old Story

The Woodcutter

Once upon a time there lived a man who cut trees for a living. He was a big man, strong as an axe, and everyone called him the woodcutter. On account of his strength no one expected him to be clever, not even himself. But he was clever and before long he was engaged to marry the miller's daughter. She was a plain girl but a fine catch. There was only one problem. The woodcutter was afraid the miller's daughter would hear the story of his grandmother in the village. She had of course heard the story before, a hundred times, but no one ever really hears a story until they need to. The woodcutter worried that the miller's daughter would break the engagement. His fear kept him up at night. He knew that the only way to sleep soundly was to tell the story to the miller's daughter himself. And so he did.

The Story the Woodcutter told
the Miller's Daughter

A long time ago there lived a young woman who was married and had a child in a cradle. One day she went walking alone in the forest. Darkness fell and the woman realised that she had strayed far from home. A wolf appeared. He attacked the woman, scraping his paw down one side of her face and scarring her forever, but luckily she managed to run away. When she arrived home her husband could not bear to look at her and shortly afterwards he disappeared and was never heard of again. The woman moved into an old run-down cottage on the edge of the village and took in washing to earn enough money to feed herself and her child. At first the villagers were generous towards the woman, bringing her lightly soiled clothes and paying her well, but later, galled by her refusal to engage in self-pity, they turned against her and brought her their stained underclothes and bedsheets and haggled over payment. The woman's child, a girl, soon grew up and married and had a child in a cradle. But, when her husband heard the story of the wolf, he too disappeared and was never heard from again.

The Grandmother

When he reached the end of the story, the woodcutter, as you might expect, revealed that the woman

14

walking in the forest was in fact his grandmother and his own mother was her child. The miller's daughter was delighted. And because she was delighted, the woodcutter too was delighted. However, lying in bed that night, unable to sleep, his thoughts turned to the story he had not told. To free himself of such thoughts he did what most people do. He told himself a much more pleasant story, about a girl who fell in love with a wolf, putting in plenty of red and pink detail, until he attained the relief such storytelling usually brings. And then he fell asleep.

The Clever Girl

The woodcutter and the miller's daughter were married. They were blessed with three boys, strong as axes, and one clever girl. Apart from the nightly tossing and turning in bed, the woodcutter was content, and in the evenings he enjoyed telling stories by the fire. The clever girl preferred stories about real people and real life but her father preferred the once upon a time kind, favouring variations on a theme involving a hero who escaped a lowly past to live a life of good fortune. Years went by. The strong boys grew up to cut wood for a living while the clever girl walked in the forest, the only thing her father had forbidden her to do. They very nearly lived happily ever after. Except that one day the clever girl disappeared and was never heard from again. The story in the village was that she had run away with a wolf.

The Story

When it is too late we all want to tell the whole story. And so it was with the woodcutter. Broken-hearted, he went to see the priest with the intention of pouring it all out, every last drop of the story, so that at last he would be able to sleep at night. And so he did.

The Story the Woodcutter told the Priest

My grandmother was a black-eyed woman. I grew up not far from her cottage on the edge of the village but I hardly knew her. She kept to herself. From time to time my mother sent me to her cottage on errands and each time my grandmother would invite me in, sit me at the table, serve me stale bread and a glass of sour milk, and then tell me to go. There was never any fire in my grandmother's cottage. Just a grate with smoke in it. On the dresser, a few assorted cups and plates. A withered piece of fruit in a bowl. An ancient metal tea caddy with a small wooden spoon attached to it by a string. Rolled-up newspaper plugged gaps in the floor. A kerosene lamp flickered in the corner. There were no pictures. The story in the village was that my grandmother had once been attacked by a wolf and had scars all over her body. My mother would never tell me if the story was true or not but everywhere I went as a child I heard wolf whistles.

The Priest

The priest listened quietly. He said nothing. When the man left he opened a drawer in his desk and took out a folded yellow page. Years before when he was a young curate and easily shocked, he had visited the woodcutter's grandmother on her deathbed. When he arrived she was very weak and her mind was running like an old clock, too fast and too slow, but he swore to her that he would write down what she said, word for word, as best as he could. And he did.

The Story the Grandmother told the Priest

Night falls differently in forests. Darkness pauses at the tops of trees and then drops thick and heavy like a guillotine. It was in that time when charcoal smudges the last light that I first saw the wolf. He smelled like a butcher's shop. Sharp. Old blood soaked in sawdust. The more you inhale the less you smell, but when you relax your nostrils they are flooded with it. When I saw the wolf I closed my eyes and circled my hands around the trunk of a tree, strong and rough against the smoothness of my skin. I hated my husband. Putty fingers. Shallow eyes. Mouth made for eating dead things. I wanted the wolf. Each day I went further into the forest. Sometimes I saw him. Shadow in trees. A creature of habit. It could have gone on forever. Always longing. Never reaching. But one evening, just before night fell, I heard the cry. There was a strange swelling in the forest, dark and malevolent. Above my head branches bent and groaned. Faster and faster I ran. My breath in and out like frozen waves.

When I found the wolf I forced the metal from his flesh and carried him back to the den. I nursed him. Sad eyes and a smell like old rain. Then I seduced him. Slow strokes of bristled fur, my lips on the inside velvet of his ear. Days of hunting, killing, eating. Reading newspapers. Winding clocks. Lighting lamps. Smoking by the fire. The way we curled together to sleep. When the men came I said nothing. I watched the wolf close his mind. I think he drooled. I said nothing when the men looked at me in my petticoat. They killed the wolf. Spots of blood on my petticoat. His tail hacked off to be nailed to the wall in the jailhouse. My husband couldn't look at me but he wanted me harder than before. Later I stole the wolf's tail from the jailhouse and sewed it to my skin under my breasts where no one could see it. One stitch every day, each one weeping and bleeding, scabbing and healing, until the tail and my flesh became one and my husband disappeared.

The End

The priest tore up the yellow page and threw it in the fire. Although it was late he put on his coat and hat and left the house, walking out past grocery stores, empty bars, villagers with shallow eyes. Mud. The earth hardened and raw. Cattle moaning low in far fields. A dog barking. Wind rattling the houses of the poor. Through the fumes of memory and out the other side of dream. On and on beyond the black trees until the sky was as white as silence.

The Palace

The palace was sick. No one believed it, but it was true.

The first symptoms appeared in the bricks at the top of the tower. A dark discolouration spread through them and they became chalky in texture and began to crumble. Architects were called in. They had never seen anything like it before and had no idea what to do. When it became clear that the discolouration was spreading, the king took action. The upper section of the tower was removed—at least three metres of it—and the remaining stone was painted with a powerful chemical seal. The tower did not look as stately as it had before, but people got used to it. The king gave a great speech. I don't remember all of it, but he finished by saying that a limb is not the body and that the whole is more than the sum of its parts. Everyone cheered wildly and waved flags and the incident with the tower was soon forgotten.

This was in spring.

The next outbreak of symptoms occurred in summer. The water in the ornamental pond became rancid and all the fish died. The smell in the park was unbearable and people began to wear masks over their mouths. The king gave the order to drain the pond and fill it with a white chemical substance. Afterwards he made a good speech about the necessity of plucking weeds so that flowers can grow. Everyone clapped but an unpleasant smell lingered in the air and the playground that the king had built was under-utilised.

My wife dates our own trouble from that time, but I think this is an exaggeration.

No one had yet made the connection between the crumbling tower and the rancid ornamental pond. They were still viewed as two separate incidents.

In autumn the sickness spread. The marble pillars in the cloister began to tilt and had to be demolished before they fell over and killed someone. After that the statues in the great hall became mottled with cankers that were unresponsive to treatment. They were removed. A rumour spread that the king was superstitious about destroying the statues—they were all of his ancestors—and so he had them sealed up in a specially constructed steel sarcophagus. I don't know if this is true, but after that the situation deteriorated. The queen's salon was blown up in a controlled explosion. A maid said that she had seen snakes writhing under the bed, but a committee of investigation cast doubts on her testimony. It was claimed that the maid sought personal publicity in the media. Likewise, the statues above the windows of the exterior of the palace were sprayed with a chemical following reports of desiccation. Unfortunately the chemical spray contained high doses of acid that dissolved the features of the statuary into gelatinous lumps.

Soon reports of the sickness were breaking in the news on a daily basis. The king gave a rousing speech about battling the forces of evil that had created the sickness and people screamed 'Long live the King' until they were hoarse. Video screens were set up all over the palace so that everyone could watch the battle being waged on the sickness.

*

My wife and I visited a therapist who asked us to write down on a piece of paper what would make us happy. We then had to show each other the pieces of paper. My wife wrote *meaning* and I wrote *money*.

After the central gallery was razed, I lost interest in the sickness. Many people believed that the central gallery had not been sick at all but was razed because the queen disliked the furnishings, tapestries and silverware that adorned it. They had been selected by the previous queen, the king's mother. I don't know if this is true. My time was taken up with the price of bread—which had gone up again—and the difficulty of commuting to work when so many roads within the inner and outer limits of the palace were closed. Not to mention the trouble with my wife.

The king made more speeches, but each one contradicted the previous one. At the height of winter, when snow and ice covered the ground and a record number of people had been admitted to hospital, the queen gave birth to twins, a girl and a boy. Photographs of the king and queen with the tiny prince and princess flashed out from the screens that had been erected all over the palace. Everyone was delighted. The king began giving televised messages instead of speeches. He wore casual clothes and spoke on topics such as male grooming and golf. Sometimes the queen also gave televised messages. She was a keen amateur pastry chef and an advocate for animal rights.

Soon after that I got a promotion at work and I joined the local golf club. My wife signed up for cookery classes and began volunteering one day a week at the cat sanctuary. Before we knew it, our trouble had disappeared—well maybe not *disappeared*—but we stopped worrying about it as much as we used to.

Spring came again. The great hall collapsed overnight, killing three and wounding seven. The next day the refurbished central gallery was opened to the public. My wife and I went to see it. We had lunch in the garden in the newly named People's Pavilion. I had *Ultimate Roast Chicken*. It was high in calories, but I didn't mind as I had been to the gym that morning. My wife had the *Green Salad with Option of Tuna*. She said it was excellent. On the way home we glimpsed the queen in one of the upper windows. We reckoned she was probably in the nursery putting the twins to bed. I said her hair looked glamorous and my wife informed me that it was called an upstyle.

No one mentions the sickness anymore. Some people say it is worse beyond the outer limits of the palace, but there are always those who like to take a negative view.

The Death of Actaeon

Chapter One

A woman rents a run-down cottage in the countryside in Wales. She's in her mid-forties and has had a difficult life but is determined to make a fresh start. The woman has very little money but she's resourceful. She makes the cottage pleasant, painting the walls yellow, sewing curtains, digging a vegetable patch and making a hen run out of old fencing. She has a girl with her of about six.

Chapter Two

Once a month the farmer who owns the cottage calls by to collect the rent. He lives in a modern bungalow two miles away. He calls late at night, when the girl is asleep, so that he and the woman can have sex. When the woman first suggested that they have sex in exchange for lower rent, the farmer was reluctant, but he soon got used to the idea. After all, 'Wales is full of such hippy-types from London with loose morals and colourful scarves.' The farmer is married with two sons, one at university and the other, a boy of seventeen with special needs, at home.

Chapter Three

The woman and the farmer settle into a rhythm. Once a month he calls to the cottage. They drink a glass of wine, chat about the weather and have sex. Afterwards the woman takes banknotes from a drawer in the kitchen and gives them to the farmer, who slips them into his pocket. He says nothing but stares at the woman's face for a long time before going out to his car and starting the engine. The woman stands still, in the kitchen, listening until the purling of the engine has disappeared in the darkness.

Chapter Four

Life in the run-down cottage is busy. Growing vegetables in the garden in the summer, feeding the hens and collecting their eggs, cooking, walking the girl to school and back, chopping firewood in winter. The woman often feels tired, but also peaceful. She knows that life can't go on like this forever, and yet she hopes it will. At night, when the girl's in bed, she smokes a joint. She has a cannabis plant hidden among the tomatoes growing in the polytunnel. The woman is not religious, but in the expansion that comes with intoxication she sometimes thinks that she'd like to paint a picture or write something down or maybe dance naked around a fire. She stares up at the sky and is comforted by the black vastness of it. In the mornings when she steps outside to feed the hens, the world appears, even in rain, unbearably beautiful, and her desire in these moments to take care of the girl is immense, to get one damn thing right in her whole life.

Chapter Five

Five years pass.

Chapter Six

It is summer and the days are long and humid. The farmer is getting ready to call to the cottage to collect the rent. He showers, shaves and puts on a clean shirt. His car keys are not hanging from the mahogany key rack by the front door and he searches around the house for them. In the kitchen he roots through odds and ends in a ceramic bowl. He asks his wife if she has seen them. Sitting at the table, coaxing the son with special needs—now twenty-two—to eat some more of his dinner, the wife tells her husband that she knows where he is going. 'To fuck that woman in the cottage.' On hearing the word fuck, the son puts his hand inside his trousers and starts rubbing himself. The farmer tries to stop him, but the boy hits him hard above the eye. The farmer lashes out and knocks the boy to the floor. Screaming, his wife takes the car keys from underneath a cushion and throws them at her husband. Then she gets down on the tiled floor and cradles the son who is rocking back and forth and moaning. The farmer sits for a long time in his car before he starts the engine and drives away.

Chapter Seven

A squad car is already waiting for the farmer outside the run-down cottage. He is not arrested but the story spreads like weeds through the countryside. The woman panics and decides to leave Wales at once. She is terrified that the girl—now eleven—will hear the story. She packs two suitcases and leaves everything else behind. She doesn't know what to do about the hens and the vegetables. In the end she writes a note detailing the feeding times of the hens and the harvesting months for the vegetables, and leaves the note on the mantlepiece, held down with a stone.

Chapter Eight

The woman takes the girl back to London and rents a flat. She gets a job as a receptionist in a car insurance company. The girl wins a scholarship to a private school. The farmer sends the woman text messages saying that he wants to talk, to meet, he needs to see her, he can't live without her. She doesn't block the farmer's number, but she doesn't respond. Then one day, after two years, she sends a text offering to meet him. They text back and forth and agree to meet in a hotel on the outskirts of Coventry. The woman arrives early and takes a seat in the lounge by the window. She orders a vodka and tomato juice and waits. She sees the farmer's car pull up in the car park and a man get out and walk towards the hotel. The farmer has put on weight and is almost unrecognisable. His hair is like a mane and his eyes are wild. Hunched against the breeze, he looks like a man caught between worlds.

The woman leaves the hotel by a rear exit, hails a taxi and takes the next train back to London. Sitting in

the overheated carriage, the woman murmurs, almost
unaware of her words, 'Am I to blame for it all?'

Chapter Nine

Five years pass.

Chapter Ten

The girl gets a place at a prestigious university and
the woman manages to buy an apartment through a
government scheme. Aside from work, she goes out
less and less. When one of her neighbours emigrates
to Australia, she takes in their cat, a large ginger
tom, and at night, watching TV, she strokes the cat,
stretched out on the sofa beside her.

Chapter Eleven

Five years pass.

Chapter Twelve

The woman is promoted to office manager in the car
insurance company. She has only a few more years
left before she is due to retire. She dyes her hair
regularly, but it soon fades at the roots. One day she
goes to the National Gallery to meet the girl—now
twenty-three—for lunch. It's a long journey. She has

to change Tube lines twice and walk for twenty minutes. London is cold and grey, and the woman is wearing new shoes that cut her ankles. The girl took her degree in classical studies and she always suggests they meet in a gallery or a museum so that she can tell the woman about art.

After university the girl worked briefly as an intern for the BBC but is currently taking time out, living with her boyfriend in Islington, a stockbroker whom the woman has never met. On the Tube, the woman checks her phone. The girl likes to post photographs of her life on the internet and always asks the woman if she has seen them.

Chapter Thirteen

In the white interior of the gallery café, the woman sees the girl straight away. She is wearing a red dress. Over lunch, sipping a glass of chilled wine, the girl reminisces about her childhood in Wales. She laughs as she delivers well-rehearsed anecdotes about knitted socks and cabbage and crazy locals. The woman tries to laugh too, but one of her heels is throbbing softly and she is preoccupied trying to eat the salad she ordered. She hadn't expected the prawns to be still in their shells.

*

Chapter Fourteen

In Room Six in the National Gallery in London there is an original painting by the Italian Renaissance artist Titian. It is called *The Death of Actaeon*. A cheap reproduction of this painting hung in the dining room of the hotel in Sorrento where the woman spent her honeymoon when she was nineteen years old and pregnant with her first child. All her attention had been taken up with her new husband, and so she hadn't noticed the painting. We never see things until we need to. The only images she retained of her honeymoon were the photographs taken by strangers with the Kodak instant camera she'd bought at the airport in Gatwick. In them a serious-looking young woman, her hands folded across her stomach, stands beside a bored-looking man. The couple are photographed against the usual backdrops. Lapis lazuli, yellow ochre, lead white.

Chapter Fifteen

After lunch in the gallery café the woman goes to the bathroom. She sees her reflection in the mirror and turns away. In the cubicle she takes off her pop sock and wedges tissue against her heel. There is a bloodstain on the pop sock in the shape of a rusted bottle top. When she returns from the bathroom the girl is scrolling her phone, waiting for her. They wander around the cool, empty rooms of the gallery and the woman, drowsy after the journey and the lunch, feels detached from herself, as though she has smoked a joint, something she hasn't done in years.

Chapter Sixteen

In Room Six she stops in front of a painting. She reads the exhibit label. *The Death of Actaeon*. The girl, standing to the side, pointing, explains that Diana, goddess of the hunt, was furious at being seen naked by a young man called Actaeon. He had accidentally stumbled upon her bathing and as punishment she had transformed him into a deer. The girl tells the woman to note how Titian depicts the young man in mid transformation. His head is that of a deer, but his body is still human. She adds: 'It was his own hounds that killed him in the end.'

Chapter Seventeen

The woman stares and stares. She has a sensation as though someone has splashed icy water all over her. The girl moves on to another painting and waits for the woman to follow, but the woman is frozen, rooted to the wooden floor. In the high-ceilinged room, she hears the girl's voice calling to her and opens her mouth to respond, but no words come out. Then, gradually, bit by bit, she feels herself returning to the world. Her heel is throbbing, and she has a slight headache. She turns and walks in the direction of the girl. She cannot see her clearly—the face is blurred—but the redness of the dress floods her vision, like a terrible wound.

The Show Trial

I went to see the show trial because someone said it would be fun. They said it would be fun because no one ever knew what the show trial was showing and only rarely could you figure out who was guilty and who was innocent. It was against my sense of identity to attend such an entertainment but I went anyway. At the booth I haggled with the girl until she gave me a discount on a ticket to the end of the night. The girl came out of the booth carrying a small flashlamp and led me to an opening in a large blue tent. She wore knee-high white boots that made a sound like a kiss when she walked, and I was glad I had come. Inside the tent words from the microphone threw shadows on the red walls and I had to stoop to find a seat. A woman was on trial. She was extremely fat and people around me laughed inconsolably. In the tradition of court procedures the woman wore only her underwear.

She was delighted with the attention. People spoke to her and called her by her name and touched her to show that they were not afraid of her. Their words echoed through the microphone and lengthened darkly on the red walls. The woman was found guilty on two counts of poverty—real and imagined—and taken reluctantly from the dock. There were many other show trials that night but you know how it is, a man only remembers his first.

The Story

Last summer my wife and I, along with our young daughter, moved into a house recently vacated by a man called Albert Solberg. He vacated the house because he died. According to the inquest report, he died from asphyxiation. And so the Commission assigned the house to me. It is true that I was not at the top of the waiting list, but I had a connection through a distant cousin with a prominent official in the Commission.

The house, when we moved into it, was filthy. My wife shovelled dirt from the floor and painted the walls with lime, but all the painting in the world could not get rid of the smell of fish. Solberg, it seemed, rarely ate anything else. All the neighbours said so, each in turn stopping to lean on the gate that stood a few yards from the front door, each telling the same story—about the fish and the smell and the dissolution—each putting a twist on the tale. Old

Peters, who used to work in the mines, spoke of illicit material delivered to the door in packages tied up with duct tape. The widow testified to noises coming from the house in the cold hours of morning. Tanya, who had never married, spoke of cats in the garden and children who urinated in the yard.

I found the story a few weeks after we moved into the house. It was wrapped in newspaper and hidden behind the boiler. The boiler was housed in a cupboard in the kitchen and I had paid no attention to it until winter came suddenly and we found that it didn't work. I wanted to hire a plumber but my wife said no—instead she read the manual while biting her fingers and shouting instructions at me. I followed my wife's instructions as best as I could, but whatever way I approached the boiler, I found in a matter of minutes that I felt like a boy pretending to be a man. All the while the spanner grew heavier and the instructions more strange. It was when my wife left the room to attend to the child that I found the story. I stretched my hand in behind the boiler and touched a bundle of paper. Immediately I knew I had found something, and that is why I did not tell my wife. The deeper a man gets into marriage the more he learns to keep something for himself.

A few days later, while my wife was out with the child, I retrieved the story from the back of the boiler and took it out to the shed. There I read it, a couple of pages at a time, whenever my wife was out at the market or visiting her mother. I also reread snatches of it in the evenings while I smoked my pipe. My wife did not like me smoking a pipe and so there was an unspoken agreement between us that I smoke only in the evenings and only in the shed.

The plot of the story involved a girl and took place in the time when Solberg was a young soldier in the colonies. There was a subplot, but isn't there always. The girl in question was a maid in the house of the Governor, a house to which Solberg—though of humble origins—was often invited on account of a connection between the Governor and Solberg's mother. The story contained pages and pages of how Solberg took the maid: when, where, how; they were full of gratifying detail. There were also endless passages on Solberg's hatred of army life and his penury due to gambling and drinking, but I skipped over most of these. It is amazing how many words people use; words that require a third or fourth lifetime. It is as though they believe that words are immune to time.

My wife had another child and then another. The last child was poorly and that was that, I soon forgot about the story. The child could not walk and spent all day in a cart made from railway sleepers. Life was hard, but it was hard for everybody. Old Peters died of drink; he was found lying face down on his own kitchen floor. The widow went to live with her daughter in a one-room flat in the city, and Tanya married a man with eight children. Over time my wife's face knotted like the branch of a tree and there was an unspoken agreement between us that there would be no more children. I gave up smoking my pipe. Each evening I carried the crippled child to bed and played my whistle for him—he took great pleasure in music—but, while still a boy, he died. I carried him to the doctor's house, but it was too late. His body, in my arms, felt like a large kitten, all knuckle and bone in a soft sack.

One night, a few months after that, I lifted the blankets to look at my wife as she lay in bed. Her soft susurrations had aroused my needs and I wanted desperately to see the shape of a woman. My wife awoke and, with her finger, drew an imaginary line down the middle of the sheet. I said nothing.

When spring came I started smoking again. I developed the habit of going out to the shed in the evenings to play my whistle and to read the newspaper, and this was when I found the story once more. It was in a wooden crate along with an old picture frame and a brass candelabrum that had been given to my wife by her stepfather. The story was still wrapped in newspaper but I had forgotten what it was until I saw the familiar typeface of the front cover:

A Soldier's Story

By Albert Solberg

I opened the story without curiosity. I did not remember much of the detail, but I remembered its flavour, and it was one I had lost appetite for. I leafed through it and was about to wrap it up again in the newspaper when a single page fell out, one I had not seen before. This is what it said:

Last Statement of Albert Solberg

Only a rare individual can love another person in real time and so the next time I fell in love was twenty years after the events of this story. One afternoon last spring I sat on a park bench and fell in love with the maid that I knew when I was in my twenties and a soldier in the colonies; a woman that I cast off, as one does a winter coat when spring appears. The feeling was intense. I have nothing more to say. I despise the man who sets the past in print and calls it truth.

I have never loved a woman, but in that instant I too felt the loss of a woman I had once loved. How can that be? How can a heart be made sore by that which it does not know?

The Celebration

The problems began the day before the celebration. I had just come home from boarding school when Father took me aside and told me that Mother was up to her old antics, letting the whole family down, and that if she continued, we'd have to act. Father was wearing a plaid shirt and tan trousers. He said that at times like these we men had to stick together. I assured him that he could count on me and, over a lunch of cold pheasant and plums, a plan was worked out whereby one of us would keep an eye on Mother while the other supervised the preparations for the celebration. It was on the second switch over of the evening, when it was my turn to keep an eye on Mother, that, exactly as Father had predicted, she began to play up, dancing in the living room, kicking her legs and almost shouting out the chorus of a ridiculous pop song, her slip showing underneath her tweed skirt.

Straightaway I sent the agreed signal to Father and together we crowded Mother to the edge of the patterned carpet, pretending we too were dancing, and then, keeping her wedged between us, we bundled her out of the room, down the backstairs and into the garage. Mother was floppy in our arms and the top button of her blouse had come undone, revealing the lace of her bra. With his free hand, Father brushed the cobwebs off a plastic chair and eased Mother onto it. There was a ball of twine on one of the shelves and Father secured Mother's hands with it and, as a precaution, also tied her ankles. It was cold in the garage and the air was dusty. Father took off his jacket and tucked it in around Mother. He said it would be a poor show if the hired help preparing for the celebration should suspect that anything was wrong and that we should go back inside. As we left the garage, I glanced back at Mother. Her eyes were shut, and her head had slumped to one side. The following morning when I came down for breakfast, there was a woman washing dishes in the kitchen. I presumed it was Mother, but it wasn't. The woman had on a pair of lime green rubber gloves and a pink dress. She asked me what I would like for breakfast and I said cornflakes, but the woman said a growing boy needs more than cornflakes and told me to sit at the table. A while later she brought out a plate of cooked kidneys and liver. I ate as much as I could, but the liver was dry and hard to swallow, and the kidneys squirted when I bit into them. With the rubber gloves still on, the woman lit a cigarette, flicking the ash into the sink and telling me, between drags, that I was a good boy. After breakfast Father called me to help with the preparations for the celebration. Several trestle tables had been delivered and needed to be assembled in the dining room. As I passed along the hall a fur stole slipped off the coat stand onto the parquet floor. The animal's head was still on and there was a row of tiny white teeth in its mouth that looked as though they were grinning. By evening everything was ready for the celebration. The trees in the front garden were covered in pink lights and a green banner that read CONGRATULATIONS hung across the front porch. Father sent me upstairs to change into my new corduroy suit. It was laid out on my bedspread, along with a cream shirt and orange tie, and there was also new underwear, shorts rather than pants, and shoes that looked exactly like Father's. A large glass ashtray had been placed on my bedside locker between my comics and pineapple-shaped alarm clock. When I was dressed I went looking for Father to help me knot my tie. Through a gap in the curtains I could see his tanned face and silver hair in the conservatory. He was talking to a woman I thought must be Mother, but it wasn't. The woman was wearing a black dress with a string of pearls around her neck. The candles in the conservatory cast long shadows on the walls that slithered in and out of each other. The woman touched my arm, saying how grown up I was and, while Father knotted my tie, she poured me a whiskey. I had never drunk whiskey before, and it burned my throat, but I got used to it, and after a few sips I began telling stories that caused the woman to laugh loudly and Father to puff vigorously on his cigar. When the guests arrived, Father told me to greet them and take their coats. By the time I entered the dining room the only seat left was at a table with two maiden aunts who looked like very old dolls, an uncle who had lost a leg in the war, and various second cousins who were absorbed with the menu. The menu was clipped to a brass holder in the centre of the table and read: seafood mousse, coq au vin, poached pears in port. Father stood up and gave a toast and while everyone was busy clinking their glasses and unfolding their swan-shaped serviettes, the waiting staff served the meal. The dining room was full of chatter but at my table the conversation was confined to varicose veins and stomach ulcers and smoking related respiratory diseases. The woman in the black dress and pearls was seated beside Father. After dessert, while the coffee and petit fours were being served, she made a rude gesture that made Father roar with laughter. As I turned away, I accidentally dipped the elbow of my shirt in a glass of red wine. I excused myself with the intention of getting some tissue to wipe the stain, but in the hall I collided with the woman in the black dress who must have exited the dining room via the other door. Holding out my shirt sleeve for inspection, I explained my errand to her, but somehow the situation became confused and she began to suck on one of my fingers. Father appeared and bundled the woman into the guest lavatory, beckoning me to follow and close the door. In the confined space, with all three of us pressed against the tiled walls, Father struck the woman, causing her string of pearls to snap and the beads to bounce all over the floor like hard shrunken eyeballs. Father told me to go back inside. He said that it wouldn't do for the guests to get a whiff of anything out of the ordinary. In the dining room, Mother was sitting at the top table laughing and joking with the guests.

Her hair was coiled around her head and her blouse was buttoned all the way to her throat. She beckoned me to come to her and rubbed her fingers through my hair. A short while later Father reappeared and kissed Mother on the cheek before taking a seat at her side. Brandy was served, and Father crowned the evening by making a witty speech in which he referred to Mother as his armadillo, which everyone found hilarious, saying what a card Father was. At the end of the night, as the guests began to leave, Father told me to get their coats and see them to the door. One of the relatives—the uncle who had lost his leg in the war—couldn't find his prosthetic, which he had unstrapped earlier because it had begun to chaff uncomfortably. I located it in the garage. When I returned to the dining room, the woman from breakfast was embracing Mother. Her pink dress was crumpled, and her nails were stained with nicotine. She and Mother pulled me into their embrace, both rubbing their fingers through my hair and laughing at some joke. Father appeared with a bottle of reserve champagne saying he always saved the best for last, and Mother put a pop-music record on and began dancing wildly around the trestle tables. Father joined in, dancing first with Mother, then with the other woman, and then with them both. The woman in the black dress returned from the lavatory with her neck bare and her lipstick smudged. Father danced across the room to her, mouthing the words of the ridiculous pop song until she began to laugh. Then he took her hand and danced her over to Mother and the woman from breakfast and, holding one another at the waist, all three women shuffled out of the dining room like a conger eel, singing along to the record now at the top of their voices. Father poured a nightcap. He said it was high time that he and I had a man-to-man talk, but I couldn't make out what he was saying above the sound of the women snaking around the house, eventually arriving back in the dining room, red-faced and out of breath, vying with one another to kiss me goodnight. Mother kissed the top of my head while the woman from breakfast kissed my cheek, and the woman in the black dress kissed me on the mouth. Feeling a little giddy, I leaned in to kiss Father but pulled back just in time and stuck out my hand instead. He shook it firmly, each coarse hair on the back of his own hand bristling as he declared, with moisture in his eyes, that the celebration had been a success. A great success.

The Love Child

Seneca was born a long time ago. He believed that the greatest obstacle to living is the expectancy we hang upon tomorrow. Because of this we lose the present, while all the time the future remains uncertain. This is the story of a woman who wasted a great deal of time (a) expecting her married lover to leave his wife and (b) expecting her single lover to propose to her. Of course, in the end, something entirely different happened.

It was an ordinary day. The woman got on a tram destined for the city. She had broad shoulders and was well dressed. She was neither young nor old but had a rich sexuality. Above her bra her breasts bulged and her hands seemed to be forever feeling their way in the dark. The woman had spent the night with her married lover, a short man with a compulsion to oppress things that were already oppressed. In the morning she was anxious to be gone but the married lover always booked rooms in industrial estates where there were no taxis, so she got a tram.

The tram was one of the newer kind and had no conductor. The woman dropped in coin after coin at the driver's booth until a ticket came out. The seats were narrow and the window was shrouded in dust. The woman did not know where she was, so she did not know how long it would take to get to the city.

This was the first stop on the tramline and people sat far apart. The tram moved as though in a dream that woke each time the doors flung open to let people on. Soon the aisles were full, and the woman breathed the breath of strangers. Rain spat against the glass in hard little spits that carried no weight.

The woman checked her phone. Her single lover would call soon and sigh loudly to denote emotion. He was young and could not understand why poor people had children or why intelligent people took harmful drugs. Through the window the city passed in a frieze of odd angles and tower blocks and statues of giants in grimaces.

A child sat in the seat across from the woman. He was three or four years old and sucked on a soother. He saw something out the window and bobbed in his seat, pointing and sucking hard on the soother. Nobody responded. The woman looked out the window and saw a plane flying low to land. 'Aeroplane' she said to the child, 'Aeroplane'. The mother of the child pulled him onto her lap. Her skin was dead from smoking too much and her jeans were empty. She looked at the woman as if to say, 'Mind your own fucking business,' or 'Get your own child, bitch.' The woman was unmoved. She did not want children.

The child wriggled free and stood beside the woman's legs, staring at her. His cheeks were glossed with snot and his hair was thin on a flaky scalp. The woman looked out the window at grey buildings merging into grey sky. She could smell bed wet. When she turned back the child was still staring at her.

Seneca said that every condition can change, and whatever happens to one person can happen to anyone. But when things change people want the past back. They want to relive their old life, conscious this time that it was not so bad. The woman, however, was not such a person. When her life changed she realised that the past is just a random sequence of images.

*

On a busy street in rush hour, the tram crashed into a bus. The bus driver thought the traffic light was green. The front carriage of the tram buckled as though made of foil and the next carriage turned on its side, broke away from the rest of the tram, and skidded along the road, slamming into the front of a pharmacy. In the end the death toll was eleven. People asked, 'How can something like this happen?' The woman was uninjured. When the crash happened, she had picked up the child and held him to her. Against her blouse, he felt like a bag of dough. She remained holding the child when she saw that his mother was dead. She held the child at the police station and in the courts and on visiting days, and in the end she held onto the child forever.

The married lover was inspired by the woman. For a short time he remembered that he too had children, and ended the affair. The single lover was repulsed by both the desire for the child and the child itself. Soon afterwards, he married a woman with a perfect hip-to-waist ratio. Seneca died in great pain. Ordered to commit suicide, he opened his veins, but either he didn't do a good job or his veins were too old. It took ages for him to die.

The Cheerleader

The cheerleader had a God-given talent for cheerleading. On days when the wind cracked stones she smothered herself in Vaseline and cheered on in the cold. Boy could that girl cheer. She cheered in nursing homes and funeral parlours and empty football stadiums, sucking up negative ions like sweets and handing out smiles like candy. Every morning she ate cheer for breakfast. When bits of her began breaking she worried that people would notice but they never did. What matter a stump for a leg or a wire hanger where an arm should be?

Red skirt + white socks + pompoms = cheerleader.

The Woman Whose Child Was A Very Old Man

This story is set back in the days when women who painted pictures or wrote books or danced on stage weren't expected to be pleasant. In fact, it was widely understood that women who did such things were likely to be very unpleasant indeed.

That said, this is the story:

A young woman who longed to escape from a dull provincial backwater ran off with the first man she met who read books and had been to Paris. He turned out to be a buffoon (surprise) and she ended up living in a dull provincial backwater with a baby to boot, a fat, healthy boy (so far, so familiar).

But, this young woman didn't (a) stay for the sake of the baby and end up being carted off to the funny farm, or (b) leave the baby behind only to die years later of alcohol abuse and loneliness. She did something different.

In the middle of the night, with very little money, she ran away from the dull provincial backwater, taking the fat, healthy baby with her. You see, she loved the baby despite the twenty-hour labour—ending in a torn perineum—that had brought him into the world.

The journey to the city was dodgy—night buses, lifts in cars, the (un)kindness of strangers—but the woman made it, and after a few nights holed up in a hostel that smelt of cat, she managed to rent a bedsit, paying the landlady a week in advance and a week's deposit, all the money she had.

But when the young woman turned the key in the door of the bedsit what joy, what bliss! (Only those who have lived without freedom can truly appreciate it.)

The bedsit was small and hideously decorated: faded flowery wallpaper, peeling in places, ancient thin carpet, a mismatch of furniture—all to be expected—but the woman was far from fussy. Only one thing bugged her. In a room with so little space, almost a third of it was taken up by a freezer, a large white trunk of a thing, the kind you find in supermarkets, usually stuffed with bags of frozen chips and ice lollies. What use had the woman for a freezer? The bedsit already had a small fridge, complete with ice box, squeezed between the sink and a lopsided mahogany wardrobe. Meanwhile there was no cooker, just a microwave, and no bath, just a table that turned into a tub when you lifted the top off. Oh well, the woman said to herself, and cleaned everything as best she could and got on with it.

Before the week was out the woman got a job in a local shop selling tobacco and newspapers to men in trench coats. It was a tiny shop, the size of a pantry, with space behind the counter for no more than one person, but stacked so meticulously that everything was in reach. At first the woman found the hot smell of newsprint sickening, but she soon grew used to it. So as not to be hit on ten times a day—having the disadvantage of being both young and pretty—she let her hair go greasy and wore a large plastic pair of spectacles that had no lenses in them. It worked a treat. (She was hit on only once or twice a day.)

There is (some of you will have noticed) a glitch in this storyline. What did she do with the baby when she was at work? After all, she couldn't afford childcare, which would cost just as much as she earned in the shop.

Well, in those first few days in the bedsit the

woman had stumbled on a solution. This is what happened (more or less):

After the joy and the bliss, worry had kicked in. Where would the woman get next week's rent? How would she feed the baby? Distracted, she filled the tub with jugs of water, but instead of hot water she accidently filled it with cold, and as it was winter the water froze. But the woman didn't notice. She undressed the baby and lowered him into the tub, all the time her thoughts flying up to the attic window and out to the barely there sky full of starlings murmuring, and when at last she became aware of sound, it was the sound of nothing, and her hands were ice, but worse, the baby was a porcelain doll.

The woman pulled him out and wrapped him in a blanket and held him by the two-bar heater and, in no time at all, the baby was back to himself as though nothing had happened. He smiled and drooled and fed and, with red-faced concentration, filled his nappy. For hours the woman watched him, but he was fine, and so with no other choice she tried it again, and again it worked. So the woman cleared out the freezer and each afternoon when she went to work, she put the baby in the freezer and as soon as she got home, she thawed him out again.

The woman never delayed, she went straight to work and straight back, never thinking of anything but the baby, even while adding up money and counting change and smiling and talking about the weather and rebuffing the attentions of the most dogged of the trench-coated men.

Well, human nature is human nature, and anything can become normal. Soon putting the baby in the freezer was part of the rhythm of life. There were no serious side effects. The baby went into arrested development while frozen, but then caught up easily when thawed out. When the woman had a day off the baby sometimes outgrew a romper suit in an afternoon or learned to crawl in an hour.

Life was good (in other words, not awful). The manager of the shop was pleased with the woman. The men in trench coats liked her and business was steady. He didn't want to increase her wages, but he did want to keep her sweet, so he allowed her a perk—one which he knew, instinctively, that she'd go for—she could help herself to any of the remaindered magazines she fancied. What a kind boss! The woman was made up. Every night, while the baby slept, she thumbed the pages until her eyes grew sore. Educating herself (just a bit) on everything from MY LIFE AS A REFUGEE to THE FUTURE OF

FOOD to THE DARK SIDE OF OBSESSION. Until one night the woman read this:

€€€ paid for short story submissions

- Aim for something light-hearted, perhaps centred around family life or a recognisable situation.

- A positive outcome is favoured, but this can be reached by a good bit of double-crossing, or the comeuppance of the "baddie".

- Be playful—have some fun with your characters at their expense, e.g. in embarrassing social situations.

- Stories may involve a death, an illness, a fear, etc. so long as the situation doesn't come across as too dark and depressing and has an uplifting end.

- Work within reality—this is fiction, but it does have to be believable.

Send your story to Box No. 9102

Writing comes with the promise of infinite possibilities, and the woman wasn't the first (and won't be the last) to fall prey to graphomania.

Over the following weeks the woman wrote a story. She sweated over it, putting words in and taking them out again, thinking about words in a whole new way. How do you overlay words on experience and get anywhere near the feel of the thing? Soon she could think of nothing else and was vaguely amazed that she had managed to live for so long (and quite contentedly) in a world that was not made of words. And then the best (or worst) thing happened. Her story was accepted. She earned €€€. She wrote more stories. She earned more €€€. She wrote more stories. She earned more €€€...

The woman chucked in her job in the shop selling newspapers and tobacco and became a full-time writer. It would be easy. She'd put the baby (now a child) in the freezer as she had always done and simply churn out more stories. But it was not easy, and the woman started to leave the child in the freezer for longer and longer. Writing was not like working in a shop. It was tricky. What felt like ten minutes turned out to be ten hours. The woman worried the boy would fall behind his chronological age, but he didn't. Something odd had started to happen. When not in the freezer, he grew quicker, sometimes two inches in a few hours. No matter how long he stayed in the freezer, he quickly caught up. In fact, the woman joked that he'd better slow down or he'd pass himself out!

Some of the rest of this story is missing, but it goes something like this:

For years the woman struggled, living on the €€€ that trickled in from magazine stories, but in the end she wrote a novel. It was a great success and won many prizes as well as making lots of €€€. She got an agent. She gave readings. She went on a publicity tour all over the world. She had a love affair (or two or three) with men who, when she ate cherries in bed, would hold out their hands for her to deposit the stones in. Years went by. The woman forgot all about her child. At night she dreamed of angels; chubby and male, naked with little wings; always laughing and playing, floating through the air or napping on fluffy white clouds.

And then one day (out of the blue) she realised that the angels in her dreams were her child in real life and she went backwards as fast as she could, taking planes and trains and taxis, until she reached the street where she used to live. The shop that sold newspapers and tobacco had closed down and the house in which she had rented the bedsit had been boarded up for years without electricity. In a panic, she broke in and ran up the stairs and opened the door. There was the freezer, its outline visible in the darkness. The lid was stiff but eventually the woman managed to prise it open and there was her child. An old man. She lifted him out and held him to her and he smelled the same as he always had, of milk and soap and early summer rain.

Did this make any difference to the woman's career as a writer? Certainly not. (In fact, it only added to her reputation.) She wrote four more novels (all well received) and an oddball cookery book in which eggplant was the main ingredient in all of the recipes. I told you. Back then there was no need for women who wrote books to also be pleasant.

For the remaining years that he lived, the woman devoted herself to her child who was a very old man. When she was writing or socialising she hired a nurse to care for him (she had the money now), and she always included him in the black and white photoshoots she did for magazines, propping him up beside her on a couch in the foreground of a book-lined room, an Olivetti typewriter visible somewhere in the frame. In the afternoons they could be seen in the park—the woman wheeling her child who was a very old man around in his wheelchair—tucking in his blanket against the breeze, wiping spittle from his mouth or crouching down close to his old wrinkled head to point out a butterfly, or how the light spangled gold and white in the branches of overhead trees.

Flowers in Water

There was once a man who made films without a camera. He was not a mad man, just an unsuccessful one. Like most people he'd started out in life hopeful and hardworking, but one misstep leads to another—you know how it is—and now, at the age of thirty-seven, he was back living in the provincial town he'd left all those years ago, making films without a camera. You'd see him tramping around, summer and winter, any hour of the day or night, clipboard in hand, tripod slung over one shoulder, always squinting up at the sky to gauge the light. No one minded him. In fact, as time passed, he was more respected than ridiculed; even in backwater provincial towns there are few who do not have it in their hearts to admire dedication.

As a young man—so the story goes—he studied film-making in the city, and on graduation landed a staff position with the state broadcaster, got married and had a daughter. He was ambitious and for a few years his goals were clear: pay off student debt, gain experience, make contacts in the industry, and then pour all his energy into his own work. But one thing tangles to the next, like weeds in a garden. You know how it is. The economy collapsed, the state broadcaster turned all staff positions into freelance ones, and before he knew it, he was scrabbling for commercials, drinking heavily and posting tweets late at night. The rest is an old story. His wife left him, taking their daughter with her. He deleted all social media accounts and sold his possessions, including his top-of-the-range camera. We can skip the details and fast-forward to a figure, neither young nor old, something spidery in his gait, striding all over a provincial town, making films without a camera.

The first film he made was of the river that passed through the town. It was an unremarkable river, brown and sluggish, a repository for plastic bags and drinking cans and old bicycles, but through his invisible camera he captured the drama of five cygnets that had been born to a pair of mating swans, their clumsy comedic exploits, the unrelenting vigilance of the parents, the oddly lyrical mood when one day there were only four cygnets, but life on the river proceeded as though nothing had happened.

The second film he made was of the residents of the town. He shot them from a height of less than one metre from the ground, panning slowly with his invisible camera over streets in long single-take shots that captured legs and shoes going about their business. High heels and brogues, runners and boots, fat legs and thin, old legs and young, bare or covered in tights, wearing jeans or trousers, moving briskly or slowly, or just standing in a way that suggested there was nowhere to go.

The third film he made was of the skyline of the town. It was—as I have said—an unprepossessing town and its skyline was without note: flat roofs and gambrels; the odd unremarkable dome, cupola and parapet. So it must have been the vantage points he shot from, or the light, or maybe the way he angled his invisible camera to create an off-kilter effect, because on film the provincial town looked like a completely different place.

But one day, when the man returned home from scouting locations for another film, his ex-wife was waiting for him. In a curt tone she informed him that she was going away for three months and was leaving their daughter with him while she was gone. In a flurry, the man tried to explain that it was impossible for him to take the girl, but his ex-wife put her finger to her lips, an old signal for him to stop talking, before simply stating the time of the train the girl would be arriving on. And then she was gone.

In a few hours, he would have to collect a nine-year-old girl from the train station and bring her to live with him, in his one-bedroom flat, for three months. Only now did he understand how happy these last years had been, living simply without recourse to alcohol, free to do as he pleased, stay up at night, sleep during the day, eat tuna fish from a can, brew coffee as strong as he liked, smoke in bed, make his films without a camera, talk to no one, explain himself to no one, bask in the failure that was his, free to pursue his dream of capturing the poetry of ordinary life in images, without that rot that steals men's souls: ambition. And now a nine-year-old girl was on her way to break all of this up. Life was cruel.

And then—like all those who are used to disappointment—he got on with it. He went into the bedroom and stripped the bed and remade it with odds and ends of bed linen rooted out from the back of the hot press. He cleared his clothes and books out of the room, mopping the floor behind him. He made up the couch in the living room as a bed for himself to sleep on, stashed his clothes in the press with the ironing board, piled his books on the window ledge, swept around a bit, cleaned the bathroom. And just as it was time to leave to collect the girl from the train, he ran out to the garden—officially the landlady's domain—and picked some of those bright purple flowers that smell sour, but not in an unpleasant way, and put them in a jug filled with water in what was now the girl's bedroom.

The station was a low-slung ugly building, and as he neared the entrance, he heard the deep tremors and shrill whistle of an approaching train. Although it was three years since he had last seen her, he recognised the girl at once in her red coat and white socks and black patent shoes; only her expression was different. It seemed to say: *Do what you like. I don't care.* Disarmed, the man made a bumbling attempt to greet his daughter, something between a hug and a grab, and then taking her suitcase and holding it between them so that no further physical contact was possible, he led her out of the train station and along the main street of the provincial town, stopping on the way to buy groceries.

The girl was not rude. She spoke when spoken to.

73

She never complained. She stayed in her room making no sound. What was she doing? He didn't know. And the bathroom. She hardly seemed to use it. Once or twice in the middle of the night he was woken by the sound of the cistern filling. Did she bathe? He had no idea. Certainly, she was always well turned out, hair combed, socks pulled up. When he asked her if she had any laundry, she politely said no.

Each afternoon he took the girl out for an hour or so. In the park she utilised the swings and slides. In the gelateria she chose a plain vanilla cone. In the art gallery, she looked hard at each picture, including the nudes. The man was baffled. He found no trace of joy in the girl. Were all modern children like this? He didn't think so. After two weeks he was profoundly depressed and could think of nothing but her leaving.

He tried to continue making films without a camera, but it wasn't the same. If he went out to shoot at dawn, he had to be back for breakfast; if he went out after breakfast, he had to be back for lunch. After lunch, he took the girl for an outing; then it was time for dinner and he didn't like to leave her alone in the evenings, and anyway the light was bad. His creativity dried up and soon he took to lounging around on the couch, reading books he hadn't bothered with for years, cheap editions of the classics that he'd bought as a student.

One day at dinner the girl pointed to the clipboard and tripod thrown in the corner of the living room and asked what they were. Films, he told her. I make films. And for the first time since she'd arrived—almost five weeks ago—he saw a glimmer of interest in her eyes. Two days later, this time at breakfast, she asked him what kind of films he made. All sorts, he replied, and told her about the river and the people's legs and the roofs of all the buildings. The girl listened and when he stopped talking she asked if he'd ever made films for children. No, he confessed. He hadn't. But never too late, he found himself saying. Maybe he'd give it a go.

And he did. He had to work to a tight schedule but in six days a film made for children was ready. He shot it mostly in the garden—the landlady was away—and when animation or special effects were required, he improvised. That evening after dinner he set up the invisible camera in the living room, and he and the girl sat on the couch in darkness staring at the wall opposite as the film began to roll. It lasted only fourteen minutes, but the girl was transfixed, and when it was over she said, Again, please, one more time, and he played it again, and twice more after that, before the girl, growing sleepy, her body sloping towards his on the couch, said goodnight and went to bed.

During the remaining weeks that the girl was with him, the man made three more films for her, each a little longer, a little more tailored to her taste. He was learning what made her laugh, what made her cry, what delighted her, what made her fidgety. The 'show' as they called it took place every evening after dinner. Shadows flickering on the wall, telling tales of faraway places, witches and princesses, foxes and rabbits, and the girl's favourite, the story of the lonely blue starfish who fell asleep at the bottom of the ocean only to wake up on a golden yellow beach that was covered in starfish of every colour of the rainbow, all happy to meet him.

And then one day a letter arrived in his ex-wife's cursive handwriting, instructing him to put the girl back on the train to the city. There was little time for goodbyes. At the station the man hugged the girl. He said she should visit again, and to write him letters, and then she was gone. He walked out of the station into the sharp breeze that heralded the arrival of winter, and home to his flat.

And that's it—not much of a story. In real life it's

hard to know when one thing ends and another begins. We are much better off with fairy tales. But since people always want to know how things end, I'll tell you.

The man will never hear from his daughter again. Although from time to time he will think about contacting her, he will never do so. Instead, he will meet a woman who is the single parent of a six-year-old boy and marry her and move into her three-bedroomed house and become a professional painter-decorator, setting himself up with funds provided by his new wife's father. The business will prosper and one day the man will buy himself a top-of-the-range camera, but for one reason or another, he will never use it. Although the initial feelings between the man and woman will fade, they will have enough in common to make a comfortable life together, for a time, but unfortunately, the boy will become troubled as he grows older, and soon enough all three will be mired in the kind of unhappiness that makes people put on weight and watch too much TV. You know how it is. When he is sixty-one, the man will suffer a stroke during a prolonged heatwave and will spend the last few weeks of his life in hospital, where his second wife will visit him dutifully. On the morning of his death, a nurse will open a nearby window and a sour, though not unpleasant smell will sweep into the ward on the warm air, wakening in him a memory of a father and daughter sitting on a couch watching images flickering on a wall, and something in him will, for a moment, come to life again, like flowers in water, so that, as he takes his last breath, he is not, even slightly, disappointed with life.

Alexander the Great

In the hallway of the house where I live there is a reproduction of a painting of Alexander the Great by the Italian artist, Pietro Rotari. It is a poor quality reproduction and hangs in a gilded frame. The painting depicts the first meeting between Alexander and a young woman he would later marry. When Alexander was a young man he had fallen in love with his childhood friend, Hephaestion. Years later when Hephaestion died, Alexander's grief was uncontrollable. He ordered the manes and tails of all his horses to be cut and on the day of the funeral gave orders that the sacred flame in the temple be extinguished; something normally done only on the death of a king.

When I was a young woman, I too fell in love with my childhood friend. That was a long time ago. Now I live in one room above a shop. The walls are painted green, but they have been painted so many times that when they chip it is blue underneath. The glass in the windows is thin. I have my own toilet but share the kitchen with other people. The kitchen is on the floor above my room and I go there in the afternoons when everyone is at work. I wipe the surfaces clean and then cook stew or goulash with dumplings or pork with rice. I eat some of the food and leave the rest in the fridge. The walls of the kitchen are painted yellow.

Alexander the Great was educated by Aristotle who, in his later years, fell in love with a boy. I imagine the boy as smooth and beautiful; soft eyes and hard arms, a boy bathed in the kind of stereotypes that never go out of fashion. The pottery of the time depicts such relationships—an older lover fondles the genitals of the beloved while holding his chin and looking into his eyes. The beloved's genitals are unmoved. He remains a perfect child in a perfect dream. Of course, this is art and not reality. Maybe Aristotle's lover was a muscular teen infatuated with his girl-cousin.

The food I leave in the fridge is eaten by a young woman from the country with yellow hair and green/blue eyes. She is a librarian. She told me this one day in the hallway. She would like to tell me more, but I pretend to be in a hurry. I live here because I have no money, not because I want to hear stories. One day the young woman knocked on my door to tell me that she was going away for the weekend with her married lover. She asked me to feed her cat. I told her I was busy. I am tired of people with their dot-to-dot fantasies.

After Hephaestion's death Alexander the Great was warned not to enter Babylon. He went anyway, fell ill there, and died; his death helixing back through all the events of his life. My childhood friend died many years ago. During the time I was in love with him many things happened, but in the end everything happened on one afternoon of green leaves blowing back and forth against a blue sky. This visual is attached to some particular memory, but I no longer know what. Alexander the Great is said to have been fair skinned, with a ruddy tinge to his face and chest, but Plutarch said that he had a pleasing scent.

After the young woman returned from her weekend I met her in the hallway. She told me that her married lover was going to leave his wife and that they were going to rent an apartment together. I expressed the sorrow due to anyone who gets what they want. In the fading light the young woman's eyes were charcoal and her hair was grey. A few weeks after that she moved out. I stopped cooking and took to eating in cheap restaurants. I rarely think of the young woman, but sometimes, when I am in the hallway, I experience an intense but short lived desire to begin my life again.

Mad Love

Not long ago, a friend of mine who had been asked whether or not he liked pornography replied that he did, but only the pornography made up to and including the silent movie era, which ended in the 1930s.

My friend is a dreamer. A lover of doomed women who ride carousels in the rain.

I love my friend. His heart is red and velvet curtains swish through his imagination.

He has never had sex. How could he? There are no heavenly creatures. No damsels in distress, no blushing maidens, no mademoiselles in petticoats. No dark hair to be let down each night and brushed a hundred times with an ivory-handled brush.

My friend says he does not mind not having sex. I believe him. I tell him sex is overrated. (I am married.)

*

My friend and I meet occasionally in a red bar in the city. We drink too much brandy and talk in sentences that would mean something if they were not so broken.

We order food from the bar menu and eat very little of it, craving only to smoke. My friend is a great smoker and I cadge cigarettes from him all evening. He understands. (I am married.)

We smoke like they did in the era of silent films, holding our cigarettes like wands and arching our wrists. Our mouths pursed into cherries as though no one had ever heard of Freud.

The last time we met, my friend confided that he had bought a peep show machine. They are apparently collectors' items and cost a fortune. We drank another brandy and strolled out onto the terrace to smoke a cigarette. I asked my friend to tell me more.

His fingers trembled lightly—one finger was yellow from tobacco—and the grey, curly ash dropped from his cigarette onto the floor. This is what he said: 'Small, transportable peep show machines were very popular in the early decades of the twentieth century. After a coin is inserted and a crank is turned, an internal light bulb is illuminated and a timer started. Numerous erotic photographs are then displayed sequentially presenting a flickering motion picture while one looks through the viewer. The pictures can continue to be viewed until the timer runs out and the light bulb goes dark.'

He also said this: 'While you look into the peep show machine, your legs grow stronger and your arms spring with muscles and your torso broadens. Air fills your lungs. Your arteries redden and your organs oxygenate until you feel you are made of iron. Your neck lengthens, your eyes brighten, your breath becomes deep and sweet. Finally, your hair thickens and your joints become supple and lithe, as though coated in oil.'

That night I had a dream.

I took a smooth glass jar, full to the brim with coins, and poured each one into a peep show machine until I grew so strong that I took my wife, stretched out in a red dress, into my arms and carried her up in the air and far away. We floated weightlessly, entwined in each other, like exaggerated dancers in an old black-and-white film. But when I looked down, the woman in my arms was not my wife, but some actress from a television advertisement for cigarettes.

I don't see my friend very much. (I am married.)

A Theory of Forms

There was a postcard pinned to the noticeboard at work. I stared at it for a long time and then, when no one was looking, I took it off the noticeboard and put it in my handbag. The picture on the postcard was of a marble sculpture. I turned it over and read the words *Greetings from Rome* written in blue biro above the signature of a colleague. The postcard reminded me of a long time ago when I had a job in a school for adolescents with learning difficulties. I was only there for a few months.

The school was in the countryside. It had once been a farm and all the buildings had been converted. The barn was now a classroom, the farmhouse a dormitory, and various outhouses served as an office, a canteen, a recreation room, and staff accommodation. The other teachers were old and I got the job only because no one else wanted it, but the adolescents with learning difficulties were easier to get along with than normal teenagers. Either they were quiet for weeks or they were in your face twenty-four-seven. I particularly liked the way the countryside blacked out at night, except for tiny stars, sprinkled like sugar, all over the sky. But nothing lasts. Actually, that is not true. Some things do last.

I probably would've stayed at that school forever if I hadn't had sex with one of the adolescents with learning difficulties.

The boy was tall for his age and good looking, but he had a mild to moderate learning difficulty and a speech disorder. He used to stay behind after class, sweeping the floor and fixing any of the posters that had fallen down or become crooked. One day I invited him to my room. I had never done anything like that before, but then, I had never done anything before.

I liked watching the boy undress. It took him ages. He fumbled with the buttons on his shirt and fell over taking off his jeans. He had hardly any body hair, just a tuft above his penis, but I was no great shakes myself. Apart from being overweight, I had pockmarks on my skin. I always undressed quickly. Naked, I felt fine, but in underwear I felt like a hospital patient.

I let the boy orgasm in my mouth, vagina, anus, whatever he wanted, and then I stretched out on the bed and masturbated while he sucked my nipples. Afterwards the boy got dressed and left, while I lay in bed, naked under the duvet, watching TV and eating potato chips from a bowl.

It became routine. Every day the boy would come to my room, fuck me until he reached orgasm, suck my nipples while I masturbated, and then leave. For weeks things went on the same way, and then, somehow, they were different. One afternoon, instead of leaving, the boy fell asleep. I covered him with a blanket and lay on the bed beside him watching TV.

Winter came and the cold air covered the boy's skin in goose bumps. To warm him up, I rubbed his back and nuzzled his head, breathing in his smell, fresh and grassy, nothing spicy in it. More weeks passed and the boy began to stay later and later in my room, lying on the bed, watching TV, eating a few of the potato chips.

Then, one afternoon, when hard snow covered the whole countryside, and winter brought everything to an impasse, from which movement, back or forth, seemed impossible, something strange happened. The boy, lying on the bed, half sleeping, half watching

TV, began to change. A thin coat of hair grew over his cold, white skin and sprouted like leaves down his bony spine. I was not disturbed. On the contrary, the changes in the boy increased my desire for him. I placed my hand on his chest, felt his heart beating beneath his ribs, clasped him to me, and kissed his wet lips.

After that, I never saw the boy again. The next morning, the manager of the school gave me one hour to pack before driving me to the train station. She didn't want a scandal. The following year I became a sales rep for a company that makes photocopy machines and married a man I met at a conference. Probably the boy has grown heavy and works nights stacking shelves in a supermarket. That is usually what happens to adolescents with learning difficulties.

Before I saw the postcard on the noticeboard at work, I rarely thought of the boy. But the picture of the white marble sculpture brought back the memory of bone and knuckle, of the soft spot at the back of the boy's skull that panted gently under my hand.

When my husband is away, I take the postcard out of my handbag and stare at it for a long time. Sometimes I stretch out on the bed and masturbate.

Then I lie under the duvet, watching TV and eating potato chips from a bowl. I am not unhappy. Some days I am even the opposite of unhappy.

The Chair

We take it in turns now.

First, I sit in the chair and my husband administers the shocks, and then, a week or so later, I administer the shocks and my husband sits in the chair. Other couples have their own way of doing things, but this is what suits us.

When it is my turn to sit in the chair, I am almost relieved. In the days leading up to it I become irritable, angry, even on occasion experiencing violent ideations. Often, during this period, I think of leaving my husband, of breaking everything. But when the time comes to sit in the chair I do so without protestation. A sensation of release and expanse overtakes me, as though I am swimming effortlessly in a vast blue ocean, obeying laws of nature that are larger than me, larger than the universe.

It is a different story when it is my turn to administer the shocks to my husband. In the days leading up to that, I am filled with intense feelings of tenderness for him. Or not so much for him as for the idea of husband. He becomes alive to me in a way that usually only happens when a person has died. Often, during this period, I find myself kissing my husband's forehead and the tips of his fingers and, when I leave the house, wearing a vest of his under my clothes. But when the time comes to administer the shocks a red-hot fire erupts in me, flowing through me like lava and annihilating any feelings of tenderness. Afterwards I am calm; even, dare I say it, content.

In between times my husband and I do all the usual things—divide the chores, go to work, come home from work, divide the childcare, go to see a movie, order pizza on Friday nights, plan holidays, talk about finance and going to the gym more often. Time running always that bit faster than we would like.

But our marriage wasn't always so easy.

In the early years, it was mostly me sitting in the chair and my husband administering the shocks, and then, after the babies were born, it was mostly my husband in the chair and me administering the shocks. It takes time to establish a pattern that works for both people in a relationship.

I have heard of couples abandoning the chair completely. It's all the rage in some circles. Live and let live, I say, but I cannot imagine a marriage working without the chair. I mean, where would the anger go? How would you both remember, week to week, day to day, what love is?

Whenever things reach a low point—perhaps my husband has forgotten to do the dishes or I have been fantasising about having sex with a colleague—I think about one time, a few years ago, when my husband was in the chair. I had just administered the last shock and was about to untie the restraints, when I noticed the thinnest trickle of blood coming from his ear. Things like that aren't meant to happen of course, but nothing is perfect, not even the chair. With my finger I traced the thin line of blood from ear to jawline and then, absently, put my finger in my mouth and tasted all the beauty and pain of the world that has ever existed, from beginning to end, in one burst of metallic cherries. You don't forget a thing like that.

Blue

One day you wake up and notice that your right ankle is blue. Your husband claims you are seeing things. You think about changing your life, but instead you have an affair with a man from work. You buy new underwear in M&S and shave your legs and paint your toenails turquoise to complement your blue ankle.

The man from work books a table at a Nepalese restaurant near where he lives and at the end of the meal you both drink free shots of sambuca. On the mantlepiece in the man's apartment there is an unframed photograph of a girl. It is his daughter. He sees her every other Saturday and the last weekend of the month. He wants to tell you more about his daughter but that is not what you have come for. The sex is straightforward but you have forgotten how to kiss. You bump your lips against his mouth and give up. When he takes his clothes off you expect him to be blue, like your husband, but he is not. His skin is pale and firm, covered in black hairs. No blue anywhere.

You tell the man from work that you believe in marriage. You don't want your children to come from a broken home. He agrees and you continue seeing each other. In a park during lunch hour—the two of you sitting on a bench eating paninis and drinking cappuccinos from paper cups—he asks if you would like to go on a city break and you say yes.

You go to Paris and stay in a hotel on the tourist trail. In the mornings you have breakfast in a pleasantly naff bistro. Music plays in the background. Cover versions of well-known folk songs. In the afternoons you have straightforward sex on the white-sheeted bed and sleep for an hour or two. Through the open window you can smell the heat and dust of the city.

You go to work and come home from work and watch TV and sleep and take the kids to football or dancing or piano lessons and clean the house and drink more than you should and shop online and have sex with your husband and continue seeing the man from work. It is in the hairdresser's, at the weekend, sitting on a swivel chair trying to read a magazine, dehydrated from too much coffee, that you notice your other ankle is turning blue. You remember very little of the city break in Paris. The only image that remains is of lying on the white-sheeted bed in the afternoon with the smell of the city coming through the window.

Your legs turn blue. You take a wellness formula and buy expensive work-out clothes, and then you forget about it. You notice that more and more people are turning blue—young people, old people, even kids. You expect to hear commentary on the TV news or online or at the water cooler in work, but you don't hear anything. You notice that people who turn blue take up exercise—running or kettlebells or cycling or kickboxing or yoga—and talk about mindfulness. On the train home from work—your car is in the garage—you stare at a woman sitting across the aisle from you. She is wearing white pumps and a white skirt that accentuate her blue legs. She stares back at you as if to say WHAT THE FUCK ARE YOU LOOKING AT?

The man from work wants to go on a picnic or to the cinema or on other breaks to other cities. You think about it and say no. Once a month you go with him to the Nepalese restaurant, drink free shots of sambuca and afterwards have straightforward sex. You like having an affair. It makes you feel interesting. Overnight your thighs and buttocks and stomach turn blue. You look at yourself in the mirror. Your body is like the body of a person in one of those 'warts & all' reality TV shows.

You observe that some people do not turn blue. Old women in cafés wearing bright headscarves. Young men playing guitars in parks. You think about striking up conversations with them, but you decide against it. You also notice that those who have turned completely blue—like your husband—have a blue smell. It is not quite the smell of nothing. More like the smell of an empty aerosol can or the inside of a shell that has been bleached. A smell in which all the pheromones have been used up. You buy your husband perfume to disguise his absence of smell, but he doesn't use it.

The man from work becomes difficult. One night after too much wine and sambuca he says things that sound like lines from a film:

I WANT A REAL RELATIONSHIP.

YOU ONLY HAVE ONE LIFE.
OF COURSE IT IS DIFFICULT.
WHO THE FUCK ARE YOU ANYWAY? DO YOU
EVEN KNOW?

His voice is thin, as if it is coming down a phone line, and there is spit coming from his mouth. You think maybe he will hit you or strangle you or write a letter to your husband and ruin your life.

You stop seeing the man from work. You erase all his contact details from your phone, iPad and laptop. You leave your job and take some time out and then get a new job at higher pay.

Your kids turn into teenagers. Your daughter is too thin and your son gets in trouble at school. You check your kids for signs of blue. For weeks you observe them closely, but you find nothing. You look behind their ears and inside their underwear and along the soles of their feet. 'MUM', they say. 'WHAT THE FUCK?'

You are very busy with your new job and never think of the man from work. All you remember of the affair is that you went on a city break to Paris and slept on a white-sheeted bed in the afternoons.

For one reason or another you stop having sex with your husband and a year later you get divorced. You move into an apartment with your teenage kids. You buy furniture in Ikea and employ a Polish man to put it together. You paint the apartment magnolia but it soon starts to turn blue. At first you try to prevent the blue from spreading. Wherever you see the beginnings of blue you scrub or vacuum or disinfect—in the hallway where the skirting board is loose or under the sink in the kitchen or behind the wardrobe in the bedroom—but as the months go by you lose energy.

You decide to be a better parent and meet up regularly with your ex-husband to discuss the kids. One day you and your ex-husband take the kids on a family day to a park outside the city. It is a disaster. Your daughter refuses to take out her earphones and when you bring up the subject of school your son tells the two of you to 'GO FUCK YOURSELVES'. It starts to rain and when you get up to leave, the grass where your daughter and son have been sitting is blue.

The rest of your body turns blue. Not all at once, but gradually, until one day you are completely blue.

Your clothes are blue. When you look in the mirror your face has deep blue lines and your teeth when you smile have a blue tinge. Your breath is blue. Your periods are blue. Your coffee in the mornings is blue. Your car is blue. Even the permit sticker for the car park in work has faded blue. You accept that you are blue and embrace your blueness. What else is there to do? You dye your hair indigo to highlight its blueness and you take to wearing ultramarine eyeshadow and cobalt jewellery and long blue shirts over blue jeans. You even buy blue paint to redecorate the hallway in the apartment—Ocean Trapeze—but you never get around to it.

You suspect your teenage kids may be anorexic or taking drugs so you take them on a package holiday to Portugal. You think it would be a good idea to spend some quality time with them and the flights are cheap. On the overcrowded bus to the airport you watch out the window as blue buildings and blue billboards and blue trees flash by.

At the beach your daughter wears one of the six bikinis that she bought online. Her stomach is blue. Your daughter has thin thighs and small breasts. She eats very little and NEVER white bread or pasta. Your son too is turning blue. At dinner one evening he is wearing shorts and expensive runners that he queued all night to buy. Above the runners his shins are blue. Your son doesn't like the beach. He spends his days playing video games in the bar.

At night, in the hotel room, it is too hot, even with the windows open. You throw off the duvet and examine your body in the moonlight. You are putting on weight. At the buffet that morning you stacked up your plate with ham and cheese and dates and a croissant and scrambled eggs and a muffin and salmon and oranges and kiwis and slices of chorizo and a miniature pot of honey. The flesh of your upper arms has a texture like compacted jelly and your stomach is distended. You fall asleep and dream that you are stuck in a blue elevator.

When you get back from Portugal your ex-husband and his new wife pick the kids up at the airport. It is their turn to have them for a week. Your ex-husband is bluer than you remember, and his new wife is Spanish. The kids walk away from you without looking back, dragging their wheelie cases behind them. In the apartment you open a bottle of wine. Lying in bed in your knickers and an old T-shirt you watch blue images flickering across the TV screen. Blue ice caps and blue ocean, blue cities and blue countryside. Blue politicians and blue scientists. Blue rich people and blue poor people. Once upon a time—you think—people got into boats and set sail on the ocean for a new world. Tears fill your eyes and you are embarrassed, even though you are on your own.

You have three more days of annual leave so you decide to clean the apartment. You start with the oven, spraying it with a chemical foam and wiping it out with reams of kitchen roll, before moving on to the rest of the kitchen, then the lounge and hallway. The radio is on and you listen to a programme about painful medical procedures before switching to a station that plays music from when you were a teenager.

The next day you clean out the kids' bedrooms. You fill two plastic sacks with rubbish and one with items to bring to the recycling centre, mostly books. You know they will kill you for doing this, but you do it anyway. On the third day you wake up depressed and lie on the couch in your pyjamas, surfing the internet and watching TV. In the late afternoon you pour a glass of wine and send a text to the man you used to work with. You find his number on LinkedIn. The text reads:

HEY. LONG TIME NO HEAR. JUST BACK

FROM EUROPE AND REMEMBERING THAT
TIME WE WENT TO PARIS. X

You hear nothing, and the next day you go back to work. Four days later you get this:

DO YOU WANT TO MEET UP?

You feel a bit sick but you text back:

OKAY. BUT ONLY TO TALK. ☺

You meet the man you used to work with in a Starbucks on the same street as the Nepalese restaurant. You drink cappuccinos and then go back to his apartment. The curtains are drawn and you can smell old pizza. The photograph of his daughter is no longer on the mantlepiece. You have sex but this time it is not straightforward. The man has turned blue and struggles to maintain an erection. You surprise yourself by kissing him, at first like you are eating a bunch of grapes and then like you are eating a mango. You orgasm in gulps with his fingers inside you. Afterwards you lie with your head on his blue chest. Tears fill your eyes and you are embarrassed, even though you are not on your own. You fall asleep thinking about a city break, maybe this time to Vienna or Lisbon or Budapest.

Oranges

One

The orange was at the bottom of the fruit bowl. It was lying underneath two bananas and three apples. That is probably why it began to rot. The darkness at the bottom of the bowl. And the heat.

Two

It was my wife who ate oranges. For breakfast every morning she had an orange, then a bowl of cereal, then a mug of coffee. She cut the orange in quarters, then sucked each segment before removing it from the skin with her teeth.

Three

My wife had gone to stay with her parents in the countryside for two weeks, taking the baby with her but leaving the orange behind in the fruit bowl. And me. Alone in the apartment in the heat.

Four

My wife and I had argued about me staying in the apartment while she went to the countryside with the baby. She said there was no way she was spending two weeks on her own with her parents and the baby. Then I said, okay, we'll all go to the countryside to get out of the heat. Then she said we need a better apartment, one that is not so hot, maybe with a garden, so the baby wouldn't be cooped up. Then I said it was hard to work with the baby in the cooped-up apartment and it was work that brought in money. And that is how I got to stay alone in the apartment for two weeks.

Five

For three days I watched TV in my underwear, ate pizza, drank cold beers, watched porn on my laptop, masturbated, and took the dog out for a walk so late that there was no one to see me not picking up after him. I left the blinds down on the windows and spoke only when my wife phoned to ask how the work was going. I said it was going fine.

Six

It was on day four that I noticed the orange was rotting. Underneath the smell of pizza and beer and semen there was some other smell, a sweet rusty odour, like death, if death was a confectionery. I lifted the two bananas and three apples out of the fruit bowl and saw the orange, sagging and fuzzed over in grey.

Seven

I left the orange where it was and ate the two bananas and three apples. I was tired of pizza. I tried to watch TV but there was nothing on and I had sworn off porn due to my rapid descent into extremes.

Eight

On the morning of day five, I woke early. The sheet had mangled itself around my torso and my mouth felt like it was full of flies. I got up and showered and drove out the motorway to the supermarket. Inside the supermarket everything was cool and quiet, and the trolley glided through the aisles while I stared at products like they were objects from a dream I could no longer remember. Nappies and detergent and bumper bags of dog food.

Nine

In the fruit and vegetable department an entire bay was full of oranges. Tangerines from Peru. Mandarins from South Africa. Satsumas. Breakfast oranges from Valencia. Common oranges from Spain. Blood oranges. Seedless oranges. Oranges with their leaves still attached. Bargain oranges, their skin a bit mottled looking. So many oranges. I was amazed.

Ten

I bought about forty oranges. It was a lot. My thinking went something like this: I don't eat oranges. My wife eats oranges. This is my chance to eat oranges. To see if I like them. Maybe I like them. I bought about forty oranges because I wanted to taste each variety, and some oranges were only sold grouped in nets or cellophane bags.

Eleven

I cannot explain why, but when I got back to the apartment, instead of putting the oranges in a bowl or in the fridge, I filled the kitchen sink with them and let the rest spill out over the draining board and worktop. They looked nice. My wife phoned. I said the work was going well. Much better. That I'd had a breakthrough. My wife said she missed me and put the baby on the phone. I could hear it gurgle.

*

Twelve

The next day I went back to the supermarket and filled the trolley with oranges, loaded up the boot of the car with bags of them, went back inside the supermarket, filled the trolley with oranges again, loaded up the back seat of the car with more bags of them, and put the last bag of oranges on the passenger seat. The woman on the till remarked that I was buying a lot of oranges. I said I ran a small business making orange juice and that my supplier had let me down.

Thirteen

When I got back to the apartment I put oranges in the bath, in the sink in the bathroom, on the kitchen table, on the chairs, on the book shelves, on the TV stand, on the coffee table, on the dressing table in the bedroom, and in the baby's cot. Then I went back to the supermarket and bought one more half trolley of oranges. There were two reasons for only buying one more half trolley. One: the supermarket had a greatly reduced stock of oranges. Two: my wife analyses the statements for our joint Visa account in the same way that scientists analyse microbes in a lab, so I was using my own card to pay for the oranges, and it was almost maxed.

Fourteen

I arranged the last of the oranges in various spots around the apartment. In the washing machine, under the bed, along the wainscoting in the hallway. Wherever oranges fell, I just left them there. The only place I purposefully did not put an orange was in the fruit bowl. I wanted to leave the single rotting orange to die in peace.

Fifteen

After all this activity with the oranges I slept for two days, only waking to talk to my wife on the phone or to walk the dog. My wife said the baby missed me. She said that the baby was unsettled when she was put down to sleep at night, as though she was waiting for me to say the Dr Seuss poem. I always said the Dr Seuss poem to the baby at night. I was lying in bed when my wife said this, and I could see the baby's cot in the far corner of the room. It was full of oranges. It was day eight.

Sixteen

I dreamed that all the oranges in the apartment turned into lotus flowers but when I bent to smell them there was dog mess in the petals.

Seventeen

The dog is acting strange. When my wife phones I tell her that the dog is acting strange and she says to put the dog on the phone. I put the receiver to the dog's ear and I can hear my wife saying things like *Good boy* and *Mummy will be home soon*. The dog starts to bark. I feel guilty about the dog and that evening I take it for a long walk. I bring baggies with me to clean up the mess.

Eighteen

The apartment has started to smell. At first the oranges had no scent at all. Except for the one in the fruit bowl that now looks like a small misshapen rat. The smell is bitter and clean. The air feels like it did when I was a child and went back to school in autumn and opened the first page of a new copybook.

Nineteen

I read somewhere that there are five things people cannot smell if they are dying: peppermint, leather, rose petals, fish and oranges. I am not dying. It is day eleven and my wife will be home soon. On the phone in the evening with the blinds pulled up to let in the last of the sun, I tell my wife I miss her and to give the baby a kiss for me. Neither of us mention work, or money or moving to a bigger apartment.

Twenty

The oranges have started to rot. Their decay is taking place at a much faster rate than I expected, much faster than that of the orange in the fruit bowl, which now looks like the tongue of an old person. It must be because they are all touching against each other, each orange affected by the orange beside it, either all fresh or all rotting. The smell is sour but not unpleasant, like soil from a grave; not the grave of a child or of a person killed in a terrible accident, but of a person who lived a long time and was ready to die.

Twenty-one

It is nearly time to clear away all the oranges. Some of the surfaces in the kitchen and the bathroom will have to be scrubbed with sugar soap, and a few items like the mattress in the baby's cot will have to be replaced. I am making a list so that when I drive to the retail park I'll get everything I need. Gloves. And large black plastic sacks. Maybe a small shovel.

*

Twenty-two

It is day thirteen. My wife phones to tell me what train she is coming home on. She will be home the day after tomorrow with the baby. They are staying an extra night in the countryside because train tickets are cheaper on weekdays. I write the time of the train's arrival on the margin of the calendar in the kitchen. We both go quiet on the phone, but we don't hang up. I can hear the baby making noises in the background.

Twenty-three

I sit on the couch, but I don't turn the TV on. I just listen to the darkness. The smell of fermenting oranges in the apartment is powerful but I have gotten used to it. Everything is ready to clear them all out in the morning. Even the one in the fruit bowl. It strikes me that I never tasted any of them. I don't think I like oranges. The phone rings but I let it ring. My wife leaves a message reminding me about the arrival time of the train.

Twenty-four

I stay sitting in the darkness for hours. The dog shuffles in from the hallway and slumps at my feet. He is tired from a long walk earlier in the day. The air seems cooler. I sit there doing nothing, but I feel different. Like I am alive. Now. In this moment. Like if I peeled my skin off and left it beside me on the couch watching TV, I would still be real.

The Birthday Present

For his fifty-seventh birthday I bought my husband
a sex doll. It cost a lot of money, but I'd been saving
for years. I work part-time in a school for adolescents
with special needs and that's where I first encountered
sex dolls when one was bought for a teenage boy
with Klüver-Bucy Syndrome. The medication to
reduce the boy's sex drive made him sick and so the
psychiatrist prescribed a sex doll. It made me think
of my husband who also has a strong sex drive.

I am a practical woman—I wear my hair short and
don't bother with make-up—and so I told my
husband about his present weeks before his birthday.
Sex dolls are in huge demand and you need to place
your order at least a month prior to delivery.
According to the website, summertime is almost as
busy as Christmas, and my husband's birthday was
in July. The manufacturing company are based in
San Diego, but they have a European outlet. Also, it
is not just a case of clicking a mouse and ordering

one. Sex dolls are made to specification, no two are exactly alike, and there are lots of choices to make before an order can be processed—nipple preference, labia style, hair colour, chest measurement, ethnicity, and so on. More choices than when we installed our new kitchen. My husband was never a decisive man, so in the end, with him slouched beside me on the couch, I scrolled through images from the website on my laptop and coaxed the choices out of him. Some surprised me—a smaller sized breast with a darker nipple—and some didn't—Caucasian, blonde, blue eyes.

We had a good marriage, but over the years I had grown to dislike sex with my husband. It was not his desire that I objected to. I could understand that. The girls in the school where I work are put on the pill as soon as they turn fourteen. What I objected to was my husband turning me into an object to suit his own needs. In those last years I became an expert at separating mind from body while my husband panted above me—thinking about what bulbs to plant in the garden, or a programme I had seen on TV, or how to cook the leftover lamb in the fridge.

The doll arrived as ordered on my husband's birthday. I had given him a gardening book over breakfast but told him that his real present would be waiting for him when he got home that evening. I took time off work to take the delivery. It was particularly warm while I sat in the living room watching the road, and I was irritated by the buzzing of flies. It was a relief when a plain white van pulled up outside the house. The box was so large that the delivery man had to wheel it up the driveway. He had a look on his face that said I know exactly what this is, but he made no comment and I signed the electronic pad and that was that. The amount of packaging was criminal. I filled two bags for recycling.

The doll was dressed in a see-through nightdress with matching panties, white over-the-knee socks and a pair of black patent high-heeled shoes. I carried her upstairs to the guest bedroom, which was no mean feat as she weighed about seven stone. In my hands her silicone skin felt spongy. Her eyes opened and closed like a toy and she smelled faintly of plastic. I bumped her head off the door jamb but there was no response. I had installed the app on my husband's phone, but she hadn't been activated yet. The technology was amazing. The current generation of sex dolls can talk, simulate sex noises and responses, and even swivel their hips and bottom. They can't walk or make facial expressions yet, but it is only a matter of time.

In the previous weeks I had decorated the guest bedroom. Originally, it had been my son's room, but he'd moved to Toronto to set up a company marketing smart technology in the workplace. It was doing well, and Tom worked round the clock. My daughter's room was further down the landing. Stephanie was the creative one in the family and was in London designing stage sets for a small theatre company. Her room was exactly as she had left it the last time she moved out, although I had cleaned it.

I had painted the walls a warm reddish colour and bought a thick pile rug for the floor and a new cream-coloured blind for the window. I also bought an expensive scented candle and a new mattress for the bed, an orthopaedic one, as my husband suffered from lumbago, especially in winter. I lay the doll on the bed, fixed her hair and clothing, pulled down the blind, lit the candle and waited for my husband to come home from work. When he saw Tina—that was the name we had chosen for the doll—the skin on his neck reddened and his eyes flushed with excitement.

Most evenings, and sometimes on weekend mornings, my husband would visit Tina. He always sought me out afterwards, cuddling me a little if I was watching TV, or popping his head around the door if I was in the kitchen or watering plants on the patio, just letting me know, I suppose, that the visit was over, and waiting for me to say something. Was that nice, love? Good. Would you like some coffee? My husband became more attentive to me, buying me flowers and fetching errands without being asked. He even lost a little weight and wheezed less in his sleep.

I worked in the school for adolescents with special needs on Tuesdays, Wednesdays and Thursdays. Monday was my day for cleaning the house and on Fridays I went shopping. Weekends my husband and I spent together. My Monday routine changed after Tina arrived, but I didn't mind. I left cleaning her room until last, when there was nothing else to do, so that I could take my time. I'd put Tina sitting in the chair while I stripped the bed and dusted and vacuumed. Then I would place a rubber-backed towel—I took one from work—on the mattress, and lie Tina on it, and undress her and sponge her down from top to toe with a warm soapy cloth, first her back and then her front, making sure I gently wiped everywhere, before inserting a small irrigator into her vagina, anus and mouth, and drying her with a facecloth. Then I would take a freshly laundered outfit from the wardrobe, maybe the red lace set with suspender belt or the black corset with crotchless panties. My husband and I ordered something new online every month or so. Lastly, I'd dress her, brush her hair, put fresh linen on the bed and arrange her on it.

As autumn closed in and the streetlights began to come on earlier and earlier, I developed a habit of lighting the candle and slipping off my shoes and lying on the bed beside Tina, not doing anything, just thinking. Sometimes I thought about all the rooms people had in their houses—kitchens and sitting rooms and bedrooms—and how in each room you're expected to do something—eat or relax or sleep—but in this room there was nothing to do, and how nice that was, especially with the feeling of not being completely on your own, of being with someone who was not going to ask you to do anything, just let you lie there, watching the shadows of the leaves of the tree outside the window flicker back and forth on the window blind.

I was in the supermarket when I got the phone call. It must have been a Friday. I remember that the shelves were full of Christmas decorations and *You'd better watch out, you'd better not cry* was playing on the Tannoy. I was just about to take a packet of salmon darnes from the fridge when my phone rang. I thought salmon would make a nice change from pork chops, and I was thinking of serving them on a bed of creamed potatoes with maybe asparagus or tender stemmed broccoli, whichever was freshest. The phone call was from the Garda station. They wanted to know if I was Mrs Susan Nugent, if I was the wife of Robert Nugent, if I lived at Cherryfield Drive, The Glen, Dublin 4, if my husband drove a silver Toyota Mondeo. I was beginning to lose patience when the voice on the other end told me there'd been an accident involving my husband and I needed to go to St Vincent's Hospital straight away. She said a Garda unit had called to the house, but no one had been there. I thanked the voice and hung up. I thought I'd better not buy the salmon darnes after all since I wouldn't eat both, and salmon makes a terrible smell in the fridge. Then I wondered what I should do with the rest of the shopping in my trolley. A boy with bad acne was packing shelves at the far end of the aisle and I tried explaining to him what had happened, but his English was poor, and he couldn't understand, so in the end I just abandoned the trolley and walked out of the supermarket and drove to the hospital.

An Indian doctor told me my husband was dead. He spoke very softly. My husband had suffered a cardiac arrest while driving to work. He had been pronounced dead at 7.23 AM. There were no other vehicles involved. No one else was hurt. He had collapsed at the wheel while parked at a traffic light in Donnybrook. An ambulance had brought him to the hospital but there was nothing they could do. His car had been temporarily impounded. A nurse took me down a corridor and into a small room where my husband was laid out on a metal trolley with a sheet over him, just like on TV. The nurse was very kind and kept asking if I'd prefer to wait until a family member or a friend was with me, but I said no, I'd prefer to identify my husband on my own. She pulled the sheet down. Although his jaw was slack and the colour had gone from his skin, he looked as if he were sleeping. I smiled at the nurse. Yes, that's him, that's my husband. Yes, Robert Nugent. Then we left him there, lying in the white room, sleeping peacefully.

The funeral is a blur. I know everyone says that, but they probably say it because it is true. It's like being in a play. You have lines to say. So sad. Thank you. He was too young. Enjoying life. Thank you. And you have cues for entering and exiting churches, funeral parlours, graveyards, hotels. And then suddenly it is over and you are back in your own bed in your own house, except that now you are alone. In the coffin my husband looked like the corpse of a middle-aged man. Grey and stiff. He was no longer sleeping. He was dead.

Tom and Stephanie took the first available flights home for the funeral. Stephanie wore jeans, saying she hadn't anything else with her, while Tom, who had brought only a sports bag, wore a suit and dark tie. Stephanie slept in her own room, but I made up a bed for Tom in the study. I explained that some of Dad's things were being stored in his old room. I had locked the door of the guest bedroom and put the key in a secret compartment of my jewellery box. Two days after the funeral Tom returned to Toronto. His flight was at some unearthly hour, so he ordered a taxi to take him to the airport. Stephanie said she would stay a bit longer and quickly settled into her old habits of sleeping late in the mornings and sloping around the house in pyjamas bottoms and sweatshirts.

On Christmas Day we ate dinner on our laps while watching TV. I did all the cooking. After a few glasses of wine, Stephanie got teary, saying how much she missed Daddy, and fell asleep on the couch. I did the cleaning up as quietly as I could so as not to wake her. I put the radio on in the kitchen. I am not a religious person, but I like listening to choirs singing from churches. When *Ave Maria* came on, I sat on a stool at the marble counter listening to the music echoing around the kitchen, tears thickening my eyes even though I didn't feel sad.

In the new year I returned to work. When I'd come home, there'd be bits of Stephanie in every room: a hoodie in the kitchen, her handbag in the hall, her phone charging on the mantelpiece, a cold cup of coffee on the worktop, a magazine left open on the couch. Sometimes, at night, watching TV or lying in bed with the electric blanket on, I'd think of Tina in the guest bedroom. I hadn't unlocked the door since the day I'd come home from the hospital. I didn't want to go in there until I had the house to myself again.

One day in mid-January Stephanie phoned me while I was at work to say she had made dinner. She said it would be nice for me to put my feet up and that there was something she wanted to talk to me about. Dinner was spaghetti bolognese. I tried not to eat too much as garlic always repeats on me. Stephanie said that she was thinking about changing careers, becoming a dressmaker. She said it made sense to stay in Dublin and work from home. And that was what she wanted to talk to me about. Tom's old room. Since it wasn't being used—

'No,' I said.

'No?' Her voice was thin and high. 'Is that it? Just no?'

'No.'

My own voice, I noticed, was surprisingly steady, and I kept my hands folded on my lap just in case they started shaking.

'Unbelievable.' Stephanie got up from the table. 'Un-fucking-believable.'

'Don't—'

'I get it. I'll be out of here as soon as I can.'

Two months later Stephanie was still there.

I went to see a solicitor to arrange a small inheritance from my husband's savings to be released to both Tom and Stephanie. I gave each of them the same amount. I received an email from Tom the next day saying thank you. He added that he was planning to marry his girlfriend in Bali. I wasn't sure which girlfriend he was referring to, but I emailed back congratulations.

On the morning that Stephanie left to return to her job in London, I dropped her to the airport. In the departure lounge we hugged and she promised to Skype me once a week. I could smell her freshly shampooed hair and feel the outline of her shoulder blades, and for a moment I almost asked her to stay. Then she released herself from me, gave one big wave, and was gone.

On the way back from the airport, the sky was deep blue like it was full of something. The roads glinted in the early morning light and the first signs of spring were visible along the edges of the motorway. It struck me that people can stay the same for a very long time and then they can change very quickly. It seemed like a very long time ago that I had bought my husband a birthday present.

When I got home I went straight upstairs and unlocked the door of the guest bedroom. The room was freezing, so I left my coat on. Tina was cold. Her skin felt like chilled jelly. A fly was rattling around inside the lampshade on the bedside locker. I unplugged the lamp and opened the window and shook the lamp so hard that the fly flew out and disappeared into the air outside. I closed the window and set the lamp up again and put the heating on. Then I went into Stephanie's room and took an old pair of sweatpants and a hoodie and a pair of knickers from her chest of drawers. I took a pair of woollen socks from the hot press. I filled a basin of warm soapy water and put the rubber sheet on the bed and lay Tina on it and washed her from top to toe as carefully and thoroughly as I could. There was a stale milky odour from her vagina. When I was done I patted her dry and dressed her in the clothes. Then I changed the sheets on the bed and hoovered and dusted and replaced the candle with one that a neighbour had given me for Christmas and lit it. I found my husband's phone and activated the app for Tina and put it on the *Innocent* setting.

'How are you today?' I asked her.

'I am very well,' she answered.

'You look nice.'

'Thank you. So do you.'

'That's a nice thing to say,' I said. 'Would you like to take a nap?'

'If you like.' She closed her eyes. 'If you like.'

I turned off the app and put the phone on the bedside locker. Then I covered Tina's legs with a fleece blanket and slipped off my shoes and lay on the bed beside her, still with my coat on. The room was warm and smelled of cinnamon. Later—since it was Friday—I'd go shopping, but just for a while I'd relax and let the weight of my body sink into the bed while the shadows of the leaves on the tree outside rippled back and forth on the window blind in a million shades of grey, as though they were real leaves, and not just the shadows of them.

The Handyman

I

It is a dull, overcast day. A red Seat hatchback pulls into the driveway of a semi-detached house. A woman gets out of the car. She is fortyish, but youthful in her movements. She is dressed in black tailored trousers, a white shirt, and a printed silk scarf. She has not been inside the house since she left it two years ago. Her husband remained: keeping the curtains closed during daytime, letting the shower leak, missing the mortgage payments. Then he got rid of all the furniture and moved to Spain. And now the woman must sell the house.

She is here to meet a handyman whose name she found online. Over the phone he agreed to look at the property and see what could be done quickly and cheaply. With all the unpaid mortgage and other debts, there will be very little left to split with her husband after the sale. She checks the time. It is two fifty-nine. She hopes the handyman won't be late. The last thing she wants is for one of her old neighbours to greet her. The sheer awkwardness would be too much to bear. She feels uncomfortable standing in the driveway but doesn't want to go into the house alone. Her trousers, which felt fine in the morning, are now cutting into her waist. She is tempted to open the top button and get her jacket from the car, but instead she stands up straighter and draws her stomach in. In the flower bed the shrubs have died, and the weeds have grown monstrous. All that's left of the rose bush is a stump. She can't remember its name any longer. *Queen of something?*

II

A white Renault van pulls up on the kerb and a man gets out, moving stiffly. He is perhaps sixty. The woman is relieved. She doesn't want to go into the house with a good-looking young man. The handyman walks around to the back of the van and roots about for something inside: a tape measure. He has a wiry frame and the deep tan of someone who works outdoors. On the driveway he shakes the woman's hand. His grip is firm.

The woman unlocks the front door of the house and waits for him to step ahead of her, but he doesn't move, so she goes in first. In the hall, the laminate flooring has started to buckle. She hears herself saying too much already. 'A bit worse for wear, I'm afraid. You know how it is. In need of a bit of TLC.' The man doesn't respond. He stands behind her. When he does speak, he only says things that she knows to be obviously true. 'That floor will have to come up.' There is a map of damp on the ceiling in the kitchen, and he observes that the shower upstairs is leaking. He starts to cough, a low barking cough that goes on too long. He hammers at his chest to stop it and says something about having to give up the fags. 'I'll get you a glass of water,' the woman says. But when she opens the presses in the kitchen there are no glasses or mugs, just an ugly salad bowl and a few scallop shells that were once used as ashtrays. The coughing stops. 'No worries,' he says. 'I've a flask of tea in the van.' When he goes to fetch it, the woman checks her make-up in her pocket mirror. Her nose is shiny, and her cheeks are flushed. She hears him returning and drops the mirror back in her handbag. His flask has two plastic cups and he places both of them on the draining board and pours tea into each. There is nowhere to sit, so they stand by the sink. There is already milk in the tea, just the smallest amount. The woman says she doesn't take sugar and the man says just as well. He has a packet of biscuits, three-quarters gone, the packet screwed tightly at the top. She takes one and eats it and surprises herself by taking another. The man eats three biscuits, cracking them first into pieces before disappearing them into his mouth.

His fingers are stained with nicotine, but the nails are trimmed. They talk about house prices, the economy, the stupidity of the government. All the time the woman feels the man's eyes on her like two pale marbles. She finds it hard to hold their gaze. The door to the utility room is open and she sees pink pipes with their metal clips attached splayed along the floor like snakes. The dishwasher is gone. Along with the washing machine.

III

The man takes a small notebook and a pencil from his pocket and they walk around the house again. This time he makes notes. He understands what she wants, a cosmetic job, just to put a look on it for the sale. She is aware of his body as he climbs the stairs behind her. Muscular. Tensed. In the bathroom there is a sour smell. A towel left on the radiator has dried to papier-mâché. The man says that he can disguise the shower leak, no problem, as long as she doesn't run any water. The woman notices that his front tooth is chipped. She likes the way he taps things, measures everything with his eye. He reminds her of the bronze statue of a boxer she saw on her honeymoon in Rome. The figure was naked, apart from gloves and a strip of leather around the foreskin of the penis. She remembers the statue in detail. When she reached out to touch it, the guard in the museum shouted at her in Italian, and other tourists stopped to stare. She thought the whole thing was funny, but her husband had found it embarrassing, and could not be coaxed out of his bad mood for the rest of the day.

IV

In the master bedroom, the man makes a note of the damaged walls and the splintered skirting board, the smashed mirror on the wardrobe door, the broken curtain pole. He doesn't say anything. A large square of the carpet is a darker shade of beige. The woman thinks of herself having sex with her husband in the square, where the bed used to be. Lying on her side with her back to him, a position he preferred because he could enter her easily and finish quickly.

Outside, the day remains still. The leaves on the larch tree do not move. The man crouches to measure a panel in the door and the woman wonders what it would be like to have sex with him. His rough skin and hard muscles, the smell of his breath, the thick sprouts of his body hair. She thinks of his wife in a dreary nightdress and imagines the ferocity of his desire, repressed for years. For a moment she feels his hands running over her naked body, as though she were made of porcelain. The man turns from the door and catches her looking at him. He gets up and takes a step towards her. She sees the look in his eye, like a dog that has suddenly turned into a wolf, and realises that she hasn't really been thinking about him at all, but of a version of him, in art, maybe, or in a movie, and now she is caught off guard. Her mind flicks to an article she read once—maybe it was in *National Geographic*—about slaves in the ancient world. It said that there were two life-size statues of naked slaves in the Louvre in Paris, with their penises bent double and pierced with bronze rings. It said that erections must have been very painful, and that it was certain that the slaves could never have sex.

V

At the crucial juncture, as the man reaches out his hand to touch the shoulder of the woman's blouse, a grey hope passes over his face, and seeing this, the woman regains her power. She thanks him effusively for his help, and he leaves, banging the front door behind him, driving away furiously in his white van.

VI

Since leaving her husband the woman has learned a thing or two about casual sex.

In the first year, while she struggled to get a decent job, find somewhere to live, and pay the bills, she had sex with a lot of men. In hotels, in the backs of cars, in alleyways, in bus shelters. Old men, young men, rich men, students, once a guy in a wheelchair. She was seeking one perfect moment of ruinous expenditure. But she did not find it.

VII

The woman lies on the dark beige square of carpet. She loosens her trousers and reaches down and touches herself. She tries to think of the man—his muscular body on the stairs—but all she can think of is the cold bronze penis of the statue with the strip of leather tied around its foreskin. Through the window the sky looks like the sky in an oil painting, overcast and heavy, as though the day had shed its brightness, leaving behind slick leaden residue. The woman gets up and fixes her clothes. She goes to the toilet and wipes herself with a tissue from the packet in her handbag. Before she leaves, she walks around one more time, checking that the windows are shut, closing the doors behind her. She feels nothing. The house has grown cold. When she gets into her car, she turns on the heating and drives home to her one-bedroom rental apartment where she waters the plants, cooks pasta for dinner, and drinks a carefully measured glass of white wine before going to bed and setting her alarm to get up early and go to the gym before work.

White

July was hot and I was sickened by upturned flies on the window sill. I never finished anything. I started the dishes and wandered off before the countertops were clear. Flies ate the sugar. At night I left half bottles of beer in every room, read two pages of a book, ran a bath and let it go cold, while something caught my attention on TV. I wore all my clothes and never ironed, so I ended up wearing silk dresses to the supermarket. The lilac tree in the yard smelled like old powder and the high-pitched sounds of children irritated me. Peter thought I was hilarious. He knows I am cleverer than him, so he loves it when I burn things or lose the car keys. Colour began to hurt my eyes. I pulled my hat down on dahlias and could not sleep in *Orchard Green*. When I told Peter I wanted to paint the bedroom white, he grinned. Some girl told him about nesting, or some shit like that, and even when I told him again, no baby, he had a smug look that made me want to smash him.

The hardware store we went to was huge, a vast candy centre, into which we trundled, like ants following all the other ants. The car was sticky and my eyes were red from squinting at the sun. Peter ran around throwing things into the trolley, smoke alarms and rawlplugs. I found a man on a ladder sorting nails into plastic boxes and tugged on his trousers,

'Where can I find white paint?'

He came down the ladder, legs bowing on every step, and looked up at me. It was Johnny Ryan. I'd given him a blow job once behind the sports hall. He must have ceased growing the day he left school.

'Hello,' I said, trying to get on top of myself. 'How are you, Johnny?'

He mumbled something, but I couldn't tell if he recognised me. Peter was pushing a full trolley when we left the hardware store, and a huge container of *Brilliant White* sloshed around in my hands.

I painted the bedroom. It was satisfying, dipping the brush into the smooth creamy milkiness and daubing it on the walls. I liked the obliterating smell. I found a Kris Kristofferson CD under the wardrobe and played it over and over, stopping to eat only when I was starving, salads of beetroot, strawberries and mozzarella cheese. I ate out of the bowl, sitting in the yard. After the walls, I painted the skirting and the pine doors and the shelves. I took up smoking again, but didn't tell Peter. At night, when he was out, I stood at the back door and blew smoke into the sky, all the way to Orion. When Peter came back we would make love. He was gentle, never anything sleazy, and with his face glued to my neck, I admired the white walls and played song lyrics back in my head.

Johnny Ryan was ahead of us in the cinema queue. It always happens like this. You don't see someone for years and then you see them twice in a month. He was with a girl much younger than me, a bit trashy with a good ass. His hands were draped over her as they headed to some stupid comedy. After the cinema, Peter and I met up with a couple we knew from the tennis club for drinks. She was as big as a house pregnant and kept talking about it, so I amused myself by brushing off the guy over and over to see if he noticed. He didn't. In bed I grabbed Peter to make him hard quick and got on top, but changed my mind and told him I was getting my period.

I loved the mornings when Peter was gone. I liked lying in the middle of the bed, guessing the day from the light behind the blind. Sometimes I read, but words seemed to sieve through pauses like light drops, spooling to heaven, never snagging. I thought of leaving Peter, but by the time I got to unbundling health insurance and who got the cat, I was bored. I got up to shower or to meet a friend or sit in the garden or pretend to be working in the studio. Days rolled by like leaves and Peter kept talking about holidays. He got frustrated and asked if I would like to be surprised. I tried pointing out the oxymoron but his face was too earnest, so I said I'd give it some thought, but I didn't want to go anywhere, I wanted to stay in my white room.

I thought of telling Peter, 'If I break now, I will be lost forever.' But some things are never worth saying.

My hair is blonde and wispy. I wear it short, otherwise it gets in my way. I wanted to dye it, that July, a colour you could lick. I went to the hardware store for some red gloss to paint the deckchairs and saw Johnny. There was something mongrel about him, with his small head and thick neck, good nose but sloping shoulders, strong body and splayed feet. His eyes levelled off at my breasts, which are bigger than they should be for my lanky frame. I smiled, thinking of his teenage cock. He had one of those faces you couldn't read. At home I started painting the chairs out on the patio and knocked over the pot, drenching the limestone in redness.

Peter said, 'Maybe you should go back to work.' He looked older, as if the last time I had seen him was in a photo from a few years ago.

I told him I was working, that I had ideas for a new project, that to be fertile, you have to be fallow, that he could never understand the creative process. I heard my words like dredge from the bottom of a canal. I told Peter I was feeling hormonal, and he held me in a meaningful way.

The next time I went to the hardware store, I was driving back from tennis and I got an urge to see Johnny. I looked good in the car mirror and there was a sheen of sweat on my legs. He wasn't there and I wandered around like one of those women who shop all day to stay out of the house, picking up Styrofoam cornices and putting them down again. I bought a bed for the cat that you clip on to a radiator. When I got home Peter and I had a row about the cat. I said it shouldn't always be me who fed the cat, it was his cat too.

He shouted at me, 'For fuck sake, Stella, you've nothing else to do.'

I pretended to be upset and lay on the couch with a fleece blanket over me. I was laughing at an old episode of *Frasier* when Peter came in. He stood in the gloom of the TV, flickering before me. Words fell from his mouth and gathered under the couch with the dust, while I listened to Frasier espousing the merits of freshly ground coffee beans. We made love that night and Peter kissed my hair, telling me over and over how much he loved me. When I came, Johnny was pushing the back of my head hard onto his cock.

In the middle of the month Peter's parents arrived. They were en route to a cruise and stopped off for a few days. I liked Martha, Peter's mother, she was sweet, but Bill, his father, had that whole paterfamilias thing going on, annoying but sexy in its own way.

He'd say, 'I hope you know how to treat a lady like Stella, son,' and then he'd wink. Martha acted like he was a naughty schoolboy, even when he soured the mood by drinking too much and getting tricky. Peter loved his parents and was grateful to me for being likeable. On the third day, I hit the wine too hard at lunch and something started jumping in me, a hot scratch I had to itch.

'Bill,' I said, 'did you ever kill a man?'

'What do you mean, young lady?' He semi-circled his drink across his chest.

'In Korea, weren't you in Korea? I mean if someone puts on a uniform and takes up a gun, aren't they prepared to kill someone?' I looked around at Martha and Peter. They looked like we were discussing shooting clay pigeons. I had to keep going, there wasn't any way back.

'I mean, there is all this bullshit about civilisation and so on, but if some guy put a Kalashnikov to your door, it's fuck civilisation. Am I right?' The silence drove me on.

'Some loser wants to rape your wife. It's not green politics then, or who does the hoovering. You want a man. You want someone who can fuck someone up, am I right Bill?'

'You're right.' He was holding his scotch into his chest now, like a baby. 'And that's what women need to know.' He was shaking. 'Women need to know what's what when the shit comes down.'

I thrust my glass to the centre, 'Cheers to that, Bill.' I almost meant it. I went out to the hall and rummaged in the drawer for the car keys. Peter came out, shutting the lounge door quietly behind him. I said I'd been sipping the same glass all night and needed to pick up materials for a piece I was working on. Peter had a childish reverence for anything to do with my work. He was wearing a white shirt and I noticed how crisp it was. Martha must have ironed it for him.

I drove over the limit with some classic rock station playing full blast. Johnny was sitting on one of the tills, but there were no customers. I walked up to him like I was going to order a margarita. I told him about my parents-in-law being over and my husband being such a straight, and how I needed to buy a barbeque. He was grinning like he had just remembered me.

'Are those Marlboros in your pocket?' I said, 'or are you just pleased to see me?' He cracked up and so did I.

'Do you want one?' He checked his watch. 'I've got a break coming up.'

'Sure,' I said.

The yard behind the store was enclosed and the concrete was damp from never feeling sun and mashed cigarette butts were spread out all over it.

The first pull was good and we talked about school, and how life's never what you expect. I talked more than him but the first pause was like a black hole, nothing filled it. He put his hand to my head. I think he called me 'doll'. His jeans were cheap and fell away when I opened the belt. His cock was springy and cut off the airways at the back of my throat until I got the hang of it. Everything had a rhythm about it, like death. When he pulled out, I jolted. His hands were those of a too strong puppy and I nearly laughed at their playfulness, until I got the picture. He twisted me back onto the wall, each vertebra jarring against rough brick, one arm across my chest, the other digging between my thighs.

'No way, no way Johnny, get the fuck off.' But he was already in. It felt like mercury seeping up through me, and all the time he panted into my face with his big wet tongue. I don't use birth control. It makes me moody. Peter wears a condom and I prefer it anyway, no mess afterwards.

Outside the sky brooded like a vision of the Mururoa Atoll. I had left the car radio on and Jim Morrison was singing *Light My Fire*.

I turned it off, put the heat on full, and drove out onto the ring road. I had a desire to keep moving, no lights, no turns, just straight road. White walls and the way the light fell in the bedroom in the morning almost made me cry. I rolled down the window to get rid of the sour milk smell. In school, Johnny was in the dud class. Girls like me used to score those guys for fun. Tomorrow I would get a pill and flush him out. Peter would be a good father. Maybe I'd take a year off work and have a baby. I needed something to weigh me down. The light was draining from the sky, and along the highway cat's eyes blinked open, as rain spotted the windscreen. At slow speed the wipers sounded like someone giving head. Each time I looked, the clock had moved, until there was nothing left to think about. Black road, red tail lights, and line after line of white.